DEADLY INTRUDER

Spotlights flooded the room and three Vietnamese ran down the winding stairway. One carried a big chrome-plated .45 ACP; the other, two Uzi submachine pistols. Hawker hit the floor and fired two quick shots, the Colt Commando jolting in his arms. The man with the .45 was thrown backward, spattering blood on the white wall. The other two dove over the railing and began firing. Hawker switched the Commando to full automatic. He fired one short burst . . . heard a wild scream, then saw the second man lunge for better cover. Hawker caught him in middive, the 9-mm slugs contorting his body. Overhead, he could hear men moving. Then someone yelled down in broken English, "Who down there? Anyone?" The vigilante let the deadly silence answer. . . .

HAWKER Series

#1 FLORIDA FIREFIGHT
#2 L.A. WARS
#3 CHICAGO ASSAULT
#4 DEADLY IN NEW YORK
#5 HOUSTON ATTACK
#6 VEGAS VENGEANCE
#7 DETROIT COMBAT
#8 TERROR IN D.C.
#9 ATLANTA EXTREME
#10 DENVER STRIKE
#11 OPERATION NORFOLK

OPERATION NORFOLK

Carl Ramm

Carl Ramm

A DELL BOOK

Published by
Dell Publishing Co., Inc.
1 Dag Hammarskjold Plaza
New York, New York 10017

Dell ® TM 681510, Dell Publishing Co., Inc.

ISBN: 0-440-16624-1

Printed in the United States of America

January 1987

10 9 8 7 6 5 4 3 2 1

DD

OPERATION NORFOLK

one

IT DIDN'T ANGER James Hawker that Con Ye Cwong, head of North Vietnam's secret police during the Vietnam war, had become a millionaire drug kingpin and warlord on one of the South Pacific's Solomon Islands.

And it didn't make Hawker angry that Cwong still hated Americans and American soldiers enough to order his drug pushers to single out servicemen on bases around the world, supply them with cheap drugs until they were hooked, then up the price until they were out of dough . . . or dead.

And if the American servicemen didn't have money, military secrets might be traded for a week's supply of cocaine or, for the really adventurous, heroin or opium—if the military secrets could later be sold to, say, the Soviets.

For Cwong, the war in Vietnam would never be over—*could* never be over. He didn't just hate American military men; he despised them. He loathed them.

He wasn't satisfied with just killing them. He wanted to humiliate them as well.

And he made use of his drug network to do just that. Several hundred jobbers around the Western world worked for Cwong, most Vietnamese, many former North Vietnamese soldiers. Cwong's base operations bought and processed the dope, then saw it safely to the jobbers, who sold it wherever they could but preferred American servicemen as targets. Cwong's jobbers quickly became wealthy, riding in Cadillac limos, living on expensive estates. And Cwong, just as quickly, became rich, a millionaire many times over because he got a cut of everything right down the line. And with his drug monies, he reinvested in armaments. He compiled a major military arsenal right there in the Solomons, and he sold his weapons to the highest bidder—as long as the bidder was a communist. After becoming one of the black market's most successful drug dealers, he just as quickly became one of the world's largest military arms dealers. He was the major supplier of weapons to the terrorist organizations of Iran, Libya, Eygpt, Israel, and any other country that had an outlaw group whose goal was the total destruction of Western civilization.

No one ever tried to short-change Cwong. He was absolutely merciless when someone got in his way. It was whispered among the drug haunts even in the U.S. that to cheat Cwong was to invite the same kind of physical torture he used to torment American prisoners of war.

If someone did try to cheat him, he never tried it again.

But none of this angered Hawker—not the drug running or the gun running or the torturing or the killing. And yet it was Hawker who had been called upon to stop it. It was Hawker who had been ordered—secretly, of course— by the United States government to declare private war on Cwong's men, on Cwong's drug trafficking. He had been hired, in short, to assassinate Cwong and take along as many of Cwong's men as he could.

But, for all of this, Hawker couldn't let himself generate any anger toward Cwong, and for one simple reason: Anger was for amateurs.

And when it came to private warfare, James Hawker was anything but an amateur. . . .

*   *   *

Hawker's first target was a private estate on Lynnhaven Bay, not far from Norfolk, Virginia. It was one of those huge stone mansions on grounds the size of a park, on the water, built during the days when the Chesapeake Bay was the place where eastern seaboard millionaires came to shoot ducks, drink good whiskey, and enjoy their wealth.

Cwong's men had bought the place to stockpile the drugs they were dealing to sailors from the naval base. They usually brought the drugs up the coast from the Carolinas, then either into their private dock by vessel or their private runway by plane.

The local law had figured it out long ago. It had made two raids on the house, come up with plenty of dope and bags of cash, enough fail-safe evidence, in fact, to put the Vietnamese running Cwong's Norfolk operation behind bars forever—except none of them ever saw the inside of a jail. Those the judges didn't let go free on technicalities, Cwong's bank of high-priced American lawyers got off. Racial discrimination, the lawyers called it, picking on the poor Asians just because of their color—which was nonsense. But then the news media picked it up, all about the racist WASPs, and that was that. End of case, end of story.

Finally Norfolk's local cops gave up in frustration, swallowing their pride and dignity and letting the madness go on because they knew better than almost anyone else that, when lawyers and big money and the news media get involved, law rarely has anything at all to do with justice.

But then the Norfolk cops began to hear the rumors, began to hear the whispered stories of a dark-haired man who had come to town, a stranger who would take care of everything if he was just left alone, left to his own devices. And when he got done, said the rumors, there would be no drug stronghold left, let alone Vietnamese punks to sell the drugs.

The local cops liked the stories; they liked the tales of the tough vigilante who had blasted the bad guys in Detroit and L.A. and New York and a dozen other cities where the goons, the punks, and the big-money crime bosses had taken control. They told the stories over coffee between the endless duties and calls and the numbing workload.

The stories were fun, even though no one really believed them.

At midnight Hawker got into the black Chevrolet rental car and drove through downtown Norfolk until he found Ocean View Drive. He drove slowly along the edge of Chesapeake Bay, looking at the water, making sure he was not being followed. Then he saw the turnoff, the long private drive that led to the estate inhabited by Cwong's drug merchants, and he went on past without slowing. The guards at the gatehouse sat inside, smoking and talking. They paid no attention to the passing car.

Half a mile down the road, Hawker turned into the lane he had scouted earlier that day, a public access to a chunk of scraggly beach. He parked the car and got out. He wore a black Aran wool sweater against the icy November wind, and had a navy wool watch cap pulled down low over his ears. His pants were wool too, soft British khakis with plenty of oversized cargo pockets.

He wore all wool for a reason. He knew he was going to get wet, and wool was the only thing that would keep him warm despite being soaked.

Taking a tin of military greasepaint from his pocket, he darkened his face, his gray eyes peering out. Then he opened the trunk of the car and selected his weaponry. He wanted to travel light because he knew he was going to be in the water, swimming. But he also wanted enough firepower to handle any situation. For a long gun, he chose the Colt Commando automatic rifle. The Colt was really a cutdown version of the M-16. It had been developed during

Nam where a heavy-firepower weapon was needed that could be used in extremely close quarters. The barrel had been shortened and a flash eliminator had been added. The stock was telescoping; when stored, the weapon was a little over two feet long.

The Commando fired standard 5.56-millimeter ammunition from twenty-round clips. With the safety tang on full auto, it fired eight hundred rounds per minute—if you could feed it that fast. Hawker had nine preloaded clips in the webbed belt around his waist; one was locked into the weapon and another taped to the stock for quick access.

Fixed atop the weapon was the new Star-Tron MK 303 night-vision system, the waterproof version especially developed for the navy SEALS. The scope looked like an expensive underwater lens. The Star-Tron's complex mirror system sucked in all available light—from the moon, stars, streetlights—then amplified it more than fifty thousand times. The resulting image, seen through the scope, was as bright as high noon on a cloudy day.

Hawker switched on the Star-Tron, testing it. He pointed the Commando down the beach, and suddenly it was eerie red daylight. He could see waves feather on the cold, rough Chesapeake, and he could see the big cement dock-and-wharf complex that was controlled by the Vietnamese, a high barbed-wire fence bordering the property and running clear down into the water. He could see a brace of guards too, see them so clearly that he had to ignore the impulse to dive back into the bushes for fear of being seen himself.

Hawker switched off the scope, slung the weapon securely over his shoulder, barrel pointed downward, and returned to the business of arming himself. He belted a .45 Smith & Wesson magnum around his waist, put a few carefully selected explosives into his small canvas backpack, then took out the Cobra crossbow, a deadly weapon developed for the military that fired small aluminum arrows or bolts. With the razor-sharp killing points screwed on, the bolts had an effective killing range of two hundred meters and could travel a hundred meters in less than a second.

Remaining in the trunk was a lone M-72, a free-flight disposable missile launcher. The M-72 was a telescoping tube that fired the extremely powerful sixty-six–millimeter HEAT missile. Even fully armed, the launcher and missile weighed less than five pounds, yet carried enough destructive power to destroy a high-flying jet fighter five miles away—or an entire building.

Hawker closed the trunk and headed off down the beach, carrying his weapons, staying low, moving quietly in the shadows of the trees that lined the beach.

Two hundred yards from Cwong's Norfolk stronghold, he stopped and hid the missile launcher in the bushes.

Then, looking this way and that, he waded out into the water, the Cobra crossbow in hand. . . .

two

HE HALF WADED, half swam.

The water was numbing cold, rough. He had to fight the heavy surf the entire way. But it was the only way to get within striking distance without being seen.

He had talked to enough people, had done enough research to know that entering Cwong's Norfolk compound from the front or either of the sides would be tough, if not impossible. So that left the back side. The sea side. And Hawker knew that the toughest options were usually the most effective.

When he was within fifty yards of the big wharf, Hawker struck out into deeper water. He did a struggling, awkward sidestroke, fighting the heavy surf. He had planned to swim in close to the dock, grab on to one of the big cement pilings, and then sneak onto the grounds from there. But the closer he got to the pilings, the more dangerous the plan seemed. The surf was crashing into the cement, pushed by a freezing northwest wind. If the waves didn't smash him on the pilings, the barnacles and oysters would certainly cut the hell out of him.

So how would he get past the guards?

Reluctantly Hawker began to push himself back toward shallow water. Finally he could touch, and he stood lifting, rising and falling with every roller that came in, his shoulders just above the surface. Looking up, he could see both of the guards plainly: two short, wiry men in ski masks and heavy coats, holding scythe-clipped automatic weapons—Soviet AK-47s. The dock formed a T and, on the inside of the far corner, a thirty-eight– or forty-foot cruiser rocked and creaked. Mercury lights on both points of the T bathed the area in a circle of cold white light.

Damn.

There was no way he could get over the fence without being seen. And, even if he did, the fence was wired for sound as well as to a complex burglar alarm system.

There was only one way in, and that was either on the dock or under the dock . . . but what about beneath the cruiser? Hawker gauged the distance, wondering if there was any way he could make it underwater.

Nope. No way. Even without all the equipment he was carrying, he probably couldn't have made it.

Why in the hell hadn't he brought some kind of scuba gear?

There was only one way. It was risky, but he had to take the chance. Spitting salt water, Hawker cracked the self-cocking Cobra crossbow down. Then he loaded in one of the silver eight-inch arrows and flipped up the peep sight.

The guard farthest from him had his back turned, a halfhearted effort at walking the picket on this cold, dark night.

That was good. One at a time. That was best.

The guard closest to him was just lighting a cigarette, having trouble getting it going in the wind, cupping his hands around the lighter. Hawker could see the man's face in the orange glow of the flickering light: a gaunt, simian-looking little man with antlike cheeks and eyes.

Waiting for a pause in the rolling surf, Hawker steadied the weapon—he had leaned it against the dock railing—then fired. There was a *thit* sound, nothing for a moment, then the guard buckled at the waist, dropping his lighter, clawing the air violently as he tumbled over the rail into the water.

The splash was absorbed by the hollow roar of the wind and the surf.

Hawker cocked the Cobra again, loaded in another arrow, and moved closer.

The second guard had turned, suspicious, aware that something had happened but not quite sure what. He walked carefully toward the spot where the first guard had been, AK-47 at the ready.

The vigilante brought the peep sight to bear on the man's chest and squeezed the trigger . . . but a wave hit him unexpectedly, throwing off his aim, causing him to shoot high. When he had wiped the water from his face, he saw the second guard running crazily around the dock, hands clamped to his head . . . then he hit the railing, waist high, sprawled head-first into the sea, his screams lost to the waves.

The arrow had apparently hit him in the face —not a pretty thing to see.

Hawker stood in the surf, waited . . . waited for the alarms to go off, the bells to ring, for a little army to come running out, gunning for him.

But there was only the sound of the sea.

The vigilante waded down the beach, angling shallower and shallower, then climbed up the steel ladder onto the dock. He was plainly visible in the circle of light, and he knew the worst possible thing to do was to act as if he didn't want to be seen—as if he didn't belong. So he strode down the dock like he owned the place, past the big cruiser that rocked and creaked on its lines, into the bank of trees that marked the beginning of the estate.

Through the bare trees, he could see the lights of the big stone mansion glittering. He could see the dim outline of several outbuildings too. The outbuildings interested him. From local information, he knew that Cwong's men kept their drug cache in separate quarters under heavy guard. Hawker liked the idea of destroying the drug stash—or making sure it would be destroyed—before assaulting Cwong's main Norfolk force. He didn't like to leave anything to chance. And he didn't want there to be any doubt about why he was hitting the place.

He singled out a squat one-story building about the size of a cottage, made of cement blocks. The tiny barred windows made it look like a stockade. Hawker crept from shadow to shadow, taking his tme, not rushing anything, not about to make any mistakes. In his belly he felt the warm adrenaline rush despite the soggy cold of his wool clothes, the warming excitement of starting another tough mission.

A feeling that was like no other feeling in the world.

When he got near the building, he saw a man sitting outside what apparently was the lone extrance—a set of double doors, probably steel fire doors. Hawker got down on his belly and crawled in for a closer look. When he was about ten yards from the door, he could see the guard plainly: a thin man with jet-black hair, sitting with his weapon at his feet looking at *Playboy,* his jacket collar pulled up tight around his neck.

If this is the type of security Cwong's men maintain, Hawker thought to himself, I won't have much trouble at all. Hawker immediately cursed beneath his breath for jinxing himself. Although he wouldn't have admitted it to anyone, Hawker had his superstitions when it came to a mission, and one of them was never to assume it would be easy. That brought the worst bad luck of all.

Hawker lay in the shadows for a minute, wondering how best to handle the guard. He wanted information about the complex, and stumbling upon a lone guard seemed like the ideal chance to get it. But Hawker had also heard rumors about the estate's extensive electronic burglar alarm system. Was it possible there were listening devices planted all over the grounds, with a central listening board someplace inside? If so, it would be foolish to do anything but eliminate the guard right now, silently, then rig the drug warehouse—if that was what it was—to blow. Hawker decided to risk it. Why would anyone plant listening devices near a guard's area, one of the least vulnerable places on the estate?

The vigilante left the Cobra crossbow lying in the bushes and drew his heavy, cold, razor-sharp Randall Attack/Survival knife from its calf scabbard. Carrying the knife in his right hand, he crawled through the bushes to within four yards of the man. The guard was so absorbed in his *Playboy* that he didn't even notice.

Hawker stood and lunged in one smooth motion, knocking the guard off his chair and coming to rest on top of him, the big stainless-steel blade at the man's throat.

"Not a word, pal, not a sound. Nod your head if you understand."

The Vietnamese man nodded quickly, shocked eyes wide with terror.

Hawker grabbed the man's collar and jerked him to his feet, still holding the knife at ready. "You got one chance to live, pal. Hear me? *One* chance. You answer my questions, give me the right answers, I'll tie you up, leave you for someone to find in the morning. If not—" Hawker pressed the knife closer. "If not, you'll

be saying grace through your asshole. Understand?"

The guard whispered, "Anything, anything,
I tell anything, everything, just don't kill, huh?
Just don't kill," in the Vietnamese version of
pidgin English.

Hawker still held him. "What's in the building? What've they got you guarding? Tell
me—"

"Product inside. Much, many product. Heroin, cocaine, chemicals, anything. Much product." The guard whined as he whispered, seeing in Hawker's eyes that he wasn't bluffing,
that the man in the navy watch cap wouldn't
hesitate.

Hawker said, "How many men in the house?
How many men on the grounds?"

The guard, trying to stand up straight, moving gingerly against Hawker's grip, said,
"Many mens. Many very many. Twenties,
maybe. Twenties-five. You no kill, I help you,
yes? Help you fuck them good, huh, Joe? Only
no kill, yes? I use my gun, help you shoot them
good."

The little man's manner was as nauseating as
the sour smell of him, willing to turn against his
comrades to save his own skin. Hawker said,
"All I want from you is the key to this warehouse. Understand? Give me key, I let you
live."

The guard was cringing now, trying to pull away, whining. "No have key, Joe. No have key. Keys inside house, Joe. But no kill, huh? No kill—"

The vigilante shoved the little man roughly away, picked up the AK-47 that had been knocked to the ground, then got his elbow up just in time as the guard, who had been cringing with fear, threw himself full force at Hawker, the stiletto blade of a knife glittering in his hand.

three

HAWKER DUCKED CLUMSILY under the knife, just in time. The guard tumbled over him, then was immediately on his feet, crouched and ready. The vigilante, who had always considered himself quick, was just a microsecond slower in getting to his feet, and the guard got off a vicious karate kick that caught Hawker in the temple, just above the right eye. Hawker staggered backward, shook the cobwebs out just in time to parry the saber-lunge of the stiletto, and hit the guard with a glancing left hook that knocked him backward to the ground.

The vigilante kicked at the guard's right hand—the hand with the knife—and missed. The guard caught Hawker's heel, yanked, and

Hawker found himself on his back, expecting at any moment to feel the sickening pain of a blade sliding between his ribs.

But the guard made a mistake. He tried to kick the vigilante into unconsciousness before finishing the job, and Hawker absorbed two more solid kicks to the head and jaw before catching the Vietnamese's ankle, twisting, and pulling the man to the ground. Now he was on top of the guard. Catching his right wrist, Hawker twisted until the stiletto fell . . . twisted until the man's wrist snapped . . . twisted until the man's hand was almost backward on its joint, ignoring the shrill scream of agony. Then Hawker drove the heavy, long blade of his Randall attack knife home, through the chest cavity, into the heart, feeling the guard shiver beneath him, quivering, dying.

Hawker stood up dizzily, feeling sick, light-headed, almost drunk from the kicks to his head.

The guard moaned, his eyes still open . . . and then was dead.

Hawker leaned, cleaning the blade of his knife on the grass, fought the urge to vomit, then stood.

What should he do now?

The question came at him as if down a long tunnel. The guard had screamed, no doubt about that. Had anyone heard? Hawker looked toward the huge three-story mansion. Had that upstairs light been on earlier? In his confused state of mind, he wasn't sure.

He had to get control of himself, put himself on automatic pilot until his head cleared. He must call upon past experience to take over, help him go through the motions by rote until his brain stopped spinning.

He knew that the first thing he had to do was rig the warehouse full of drugs to self-destruct. He had to make sure that the warehouse was destroyed even if the rest of his mission was a failure. The guard had said there was heroin in there. Heroin, cocaine, chemicals—all of it bound for the U.S. sailors of Norfolk if something wasn't done.

Trouble was, it wasn't going to be easy getting into the damn place.

Hawker went to the double doors. He slid out of the Colt Commando, out of the backpack, and took out a little microflashlight. Peering into his pack, he pushed aside the carefully prepared explosives until he found what he was looking for—two small plastic vials. One was an extremely powerful but inert acid, the other was a catalyst. The catalyst would activate the acid when the two were combined. Using an eyedropper, the vigilante deposited drops of liquid inside both locks of the steel doors. The acid fumed and hissed, eating away the locks' internal works.

When that was done, Hawker took a long wire that had alligator clips on both ends. The burglar alarm, he hoped, would be a standard one; if so, the doors would be wired to an internal electrical circuit. Any break in the circuit would set off the alarm.

Hawker cracked one door just enough to see the conductor plates on the door seal. Then he hooked an alligator clip to each conductor plate and opened the door just enough for him to slide through—being damn careful not to kick the wire loose as he did so.

Once the door was closed behind him, the vigilante breathed easier. There were no windows in the building, none. He patted the wall until he found the switch, turned on the lights . . . and saw a single large room stacked to the ceiling with boxes wrapped in plastic—black plastic, like garbage bags. He pulled the Randall once again from its leg holster and cut one of the bags. Fine white powder poured out onto the cement floor—heroin or cocaine, he didn't know which. And he wasn't about to taste it like the TV cops did. No cop with any brains would ever chance such a stupid thing because the stuff might be one of the junkie standards or, just as easily, LSD or mescaline or angel dust. Just a taste might send you tripping your brains out.

Working quickly, Hawker removed from his pack a small slab of claylike material, top section blue, bottom section yellow, covered on each side by waxed paper. He kneaded the plastic explosive until the combination of the two colors made green, then broke it into three fist-size chunks. Into each chunk he inserted tiny radio detonating devices. Then after sticking each at the base of the three exposed walls, he stepped back out into the darkness, over the corpse of the dead guard.

The wind was blowing cold off the Chesapeake, wild in the bare tree limbs, but Hawker didn't notice, so intent was he on the house in the distance. The crossbow was strapped over his back now, and in his hands he held the Colt Commando automatic rifle.

Playtime was over. It was time to get serious with the drug pushers employed by Con Ye Cwong.

There was still just that one light on—the light upstairs. Apparently no one had heard the scream. With the noise of the wind and sea, Hawker wasn't all that surprised.

It was a perfect night for this kind of mission. It was the first of what he hoped would be many deadly blows aimed right at the heart of Cwong's empire, and Hawker wanted the

Vietnamese drug lord to feel it all the way back in the Solomon Islands.

Hawker knew he would be going to those islands soon enough, to take the message in person. But first he wanted to knock out the American franchises.

He crossed quietly through the shadows, moving from tree to tree, past hedges and marble statues, small fountains, figures of fat sitting Buddhas. Then he was twenty yards from the back door of the mansion, the service entrance, and still no sign of movement, no sign of another guard. Once again he got the feeling that maybe this would be easy after all. Immediately Hawker pushed the thought out of his mind.

He walked easily across the asphalt, holding the Commando assault rifle against his leg so that it wouldn't stand out in silhouette. Then he went up the steps and tried the door.

The door swung open easily. . . .

Hawker stopped in the doorway, looking this way and that. Guards on the dock, burglar alarms supposedly everywhere, and they leave the damned back door unlocked? That made no sense at all. What the hell was going on?

The vigilante thought for a moment, then touched the safety tang of the rifle, switching it to semiautomatic. If he was walking into a trap, he didn't relish the idea of having to reclip in darkness and damned tight quarters.

From his side holster, he drew the Smith & Wesson .45 magnum, the weight of it and the checkered grip feeling good in his hand. Carrying the Commando in his left hand, he entered the house. He was in some kind of storage area —boxes, a washing machine, the smell of soap. Then he moved into the kitchen—a big commercial-type kitchen with stainless-steel tables and hanging pots. Suddenly he heard something and came to a quick stop. Something in the corner, some kind of odd scratching noise. Hawker twisted the lens of the microflashlight and painted the beam around.

Rats. The kitchen was crawling with rats, dozens of them scurrying, scrabbling in fear, running from the light. Hawker shut the flashlight off quickly, not wanting any more noise. He put his hand on a table to find his way out while his eyes adjusted. But as he did so, he felt something heavy run over his hand and up his arm, scratching his neck. A big rat. Hawker turned too quickly, slapping the rodent off, but hitting something hard and sending a whole rack of pots clattering, clanking down on him, a deafening noise in the stillness of the dark house that sounded like the whole kitchen was collapsing.

The vigilante stood breathless in the hollow

silence. He heard a muted voice call something from upstairs and waited another full two minutes, hearing nothing else.

Maybe it was going to be okay after all; maybe these Vietnamese had gotten soft and fat over here in the land of free trade and could sleep through anything.

James Hawker made his way out of the kitchen, took two steps, and found out how wrong he was. . . .

four

LIGHTS FLASHED ON as Hawker stepped from
the kitchen into some kind of huge hall, one of
those rooms in mansions where they probably
once held dinner parties and dances.

Lights flashed on, bright burglar spotlights in
the high corners of the room, and before him,
coming down the wide winding stairway, were
three men—three Vietnamese in baggy khakis
and no shirts, with mussed hair, sparse black
moustaches, and bellies hanging out. Each of
them carried a weapon: one held a big chrome-
plated .45 ACP, the other two Uzi submachine
gun pistols.

The one carrying the .45 spotted Hawker
first, screamed out something in Vietnamese,
and fired from the hip. Plaster cracked over

the vigilante's head, but first there was the echoing *ker-WHACK* that told him the slug had passed damn close to his head.

He dropped to the floor, belly first, and squeezed off two quick shots, the Colt Commando jolting in his arms and making that tinny fiberglass sound. The man holding the .45 was thrown backward, screaming. The pistol went tumbling into the air as his face disintegrated into a pulpy mess and his body fell down the steps, splattering blood on the white wall.

The other two men dove over the railing even though they were a half-dozen feet above the main floor. They reached the floor behind a table and chair set and began firing immediately, the big room echoing with gunfire.

Wood and glass and tile shattered all around the vigilante, and he fought the reaction to close his eyes and turn his head away because, in a fire fight, as in boxing, to close your eyes is to invite disaster.

With his thumb, Hawker hit the safety tang and the Commando switched to full automatic. Seeing the legs of one of the men, he fired off one short burst. A wild scream followed. The second man rose and tried to lunge to better cover. Hawker caught him in middive, cutting him down with a second burst that sent the man tumbling sideways, his whole body contorting with the impact of the 9-millimeter slugs.

Hawker jumped quickly to his feet, drew his own .45 Smith & Wesson, and saw the wounded man beyond the table. The man looked Hawker full in the face, his eyes bitter as he reached for the Uzi that lay beside his bleeding legs. But Hawker finished him before he could reach it. One careful shot to the head did the trick, the .45 jumping heavily in his hand.

In the glare of the burglar lights, Hawker yanked free the fresh clip that was taped to the Colt, ejected the old one, put it carefully in his pocket, and slid in the new one. As he sprinted across the room to the stairs, he carried the Commando in his left hand and the Smith & Wesson in his right.

The three corpses lay bleeding nearby, the air filled with the brassy stink of their blood and the odor of gunpowder. Hawker stopped on the bottom step, waiting.

Overhead he could hear the thudding shuffle of moving feet, could hear the occasional careless whisper of men trying to be quiet but not succeeding. A loud yell in Vietnamese, sounding like a question, changed all that. Hawker heard the question again.

The men upstairs were calling to the three dead men, hoping the intruder had been taken, hoping the intruder was dead. Hawker was tempted to answer back, to yell something, anything, just to get a reaction. But he didn't.

Then: "Hey, you? Who down there? Anyone down there?" The person yelled from the second floor in broken English, his voice tentative, worried.

Once again the vigilante restrained the urge to call an answer, to taunt them. He waited . . . then heard the same voice: "You police-ee? You no have warrant, we make big stink, yes? You have warrant? We know rights, yes? We have big lawyer, make big stink!"

The vigilante let the deadly silence answer, let the silence grate at the men upstairs, knowing that it was getting to them when the voice yelled, "We kill you, motherfucker! We kill you, no chance you escape now!"

Hawker waited with growing confidence. But when he heard the hydraulic clank and whir of something moving, he realized that a house this big would likely have more than one passageway upstairs. Was the noise that of an elevator?

The thought had hardly entered his mind when two more men came charging into the room. They came sprinting through, almost firing before they jumped from the service elevator, spraying the room with slugs from big, brutal-looking AK-47s with scythe clips, standard Soviet issue.

The vigilante didn't have a moment to think. He dropped to the floor and opened fire in return, holding the Commando on full automatic, squeezing off shots with the Smith & Wesson, laying a withering cover of fire that slammed his attackers in their tracks. They were dead before they hit the ground.

Hawker turned quickly back toward the stairs knowing that, if they charged him from above now, he was dead—dead because both his weapons were nearly spent. Holding his breath in that microsecond, already sliding out of his pack, Hawker reached for the explosives. They would be his only hope.

But the men did not charge. They waited like the cowards they were, hoping their Kamikazes would put him away before they had to show their faces.

The vigilante quickly popped fresh clips into both the Colt Commando assault rifle and the .45, his hands deadly calm, in perfect control. This was what James Hawker did better than anything else, and probably better than anyone who had ever done it. This was what he lived for, tough missions in the dark of night, fighting on unfamiliar turf where he knew his total detachment and lack of emotion were the only edge he had.

Again came the voice at the top of the stairs, calling in Vietnamese for an answer, hoping his fellow gang members would yell back that the intruder was dead, the trouble over.

Hawker let silence be his only answer as he waited, the solid metal of his weapons now warm in his hands, fully loaded and ready.

Then he heard something odd. Something heavy thudded onto the stairs, thudded and rolled. He realized what the noise was just in time and dove down the hall, the stair wall protecting him as a hand grenade exploded. It was a shrapnel offensive grenade, and it brought plaster raining down and filled the room with dust from the percussion.

Hawker thought, They know this is a fight to the finish, or else they wouldn't have tried that . . . wouldn't have blown up part of their own house even if they are slobs.

But he didn't have time to think about anything else, because then they came charging at him—from the stairs and from the set of wide double doors that led to the outside, coming at him from both directions. . . .

five

HAWKER TOOK THE men coming through the door first, reasoning in that millisecond that the men upstairs were the least anxious to attack. They would probably be a few steps slower, hoping it would be over before they had to put their lives on the line.

That one bit of reasoning probably saved the vigilante's life.

As the three men came crashing through the doorway, Hawker held the trigger of the Commando on full fire, pointing it carefully back and forth, trying to conserve a few rounds, seeing the men's faces grow wide-eyed with shock as the slugs slammed home, tearing through their bodies. And in those long seconds, his back was completely unprotected; they could have taken him from the stairs at their leisure, gunned him down in perfect safety. . . .

But they laid off just long enough.

When the open doorway was filled with only the screams of the dying, Hawker immediately turned his attention to the stairs—just in time to see the feet, then legs, then body of the first man charge. Behind this first attacker, screaming wild battle cries, came four more, all firing at once.

The light in the room now was hazy with dust and falling plaster and gunpowder, and Hawker squinted over the barrel of the Commando, having no choice but to hold it on full automatic.

The first man winced, fell sideways over the railing, his arms thrown outward as if he might fly.

The next man staggered, stumbled, his white T-shirt splotched with blackish-red holes, then fell. And in that instant, the Colt Commando went silent, its clip empty.

Hawker raised the Smith & Wesson automatic carefully, held the iridescent orange competition sight on the third man's chest forty yards away, fired . . . missed . . . fired again, and the slow-moving .45 slug hit the man in the head, snapping his neck back, breaking it, and most likely killing him before the lead entered the brain cavity.

All of this happened in an instant. The final Vietnamese in the charge had decided that the stairway was not the place to be. He vaulted over the railing, an Uzi submachine gun in his left hand. Hawker shot again with the .45, this time just pointing, not aiming, and had better luck. The slug hit the man in the left hip, spinning him in midair. He landed headfirst on the hard floor, kicking crazily for a moment, then lying still.

Then all was silent—a hollow, echoing, ticking silence of falling plaster dust and distant roar of the surf outside.

But there was something else too. What?

The vigilante strained to hear as he reloaded once more, strained to identify the sound. He finally realized what it might be.

It sounded like people outside . . . like men running but trying not to be heard . . . the foot-thud of men getting farther and farther away, not closer.

He finally realized that the rest of Con Ye Cwong's gang of Norfolk drug runners were trying to flee, to escape.

The vigilante quickly reached into his backpack and pulled out a pair of TH3 incendiary grenades. There might be more men, more drugs upstairs, and he didn't want any of these bastards or their narcotic poison to escape destruction.

But he sure as hell wasn't going to let the men outside escape, because they were, in all likelihood, the leaders. And the leaders in these kinds of low-life gangs were almost always the last to fight and the first to run.

Hawker drew the pins from both grenades, holding the safety arms until he was ready, then lobbed both canisters toward the far walls of the old mansion. Then he ran for cover, back toward the kitchen.

The grenades, armed with 750 grams each of thermite, exploded with a searing white flash of streaming white smoke rays. The thermite burned at more than 3,600 degrees Fahrenheit, and the vigilante could feel the terrible heat on his back as he ran, knowing the house would soon be entirely consumed by flames.

Outside now, it took his eyes a moment to adjust to the darkness. The temperature had fallen and a bitter autumn wind blew off the Chesapeake, through the bare trees. His clothes were still wet, clammy with sweat and salt water, and the wind stung as he ran into the yard, his Smith & Wesson holstered now but the assault rifle waist-high and ready. Behind him, the spreading fire cast an eerie orange glow on the windows of the mansion. Ahead of him, he could see dim figures on the dock—men in a hurry.

When he heard the diesel rumble of engines

starting, first one, then another, he knew immediately what it was. The survivors of Cwong's Norfolk connection were trying to escape by sea, probably figuring it was the local cops or maybe the FBI who had hit them and that the roads weren't safe. They were probably going to take the big cruiser far enough down or up the coast until they figured it was safe, then maybe run it in close enough so they could either swim to shore or hop out onto some private dock. For tickets, they had probably gathered all the cash they could find—a hell of a bundle, in all likelihood—hoping to buy their way out.

Hawker took off running, running as hard as he could in the darkness, the bushes and broken limbs tearing at him. He still had about a hundred yards to reach the dock when he saw one of the men throw off the bow line and fall backward as the man at the controls jammed the big cruiser into gear, trying to speed away.

The big diesel engines screamed, and the boat veered crazily because the stern line was still cleated to the dock. But the cleat on the boat finally gave away with a tremendous *bang,* and then the cruiser was on its way, throwing a huge white wake, taking wind-froth over the bow, running with no lights toward the darkness of open water.

Hawker stopped, raised the Colt Commando, and held it on full fire, peppering the yacht with slugs from more than two hundred yards away. If the slugs hit, Hawker couldn't tell, because the boat didn't slow or serve for even an instant.

Damn it!

They were getting away. The core of Cwong's Norfolk gang was probably inside the cabin, probably still sweating, but able to smile a little bit now, knowing they had made it even if most of their men hadn't. And the vigilante knew they wouldn't give a good goddamn.

Hawker's mind raced, thinking what he might do. Maybe he would make an anonymous call to the Coast Guard, telling them a suspicious boat carrying a ton of cash money was headed south from Norfolk. The money was a sure thing. After all, it was their only hope of escape once they abandoned the boat.

But what good would calling the Coast Guard do? At best it might get the men arrested, just so some high-priced asshole attorney could get them off.

No, that wouldn't work . . . wouldn't do any good at all.

And then James Hawker remembered.

He went running down the dock. He stopped for a moment and fished the little waterproof transmitter from his pack, then lifted the safety shield and flipped the toggle switch.

The warehouse full of drugs, far back in the trees, made a *whoof*ing sound, then exploded in a fiery orange ball, throwing flames and sparks high into the night sky.

Debris began to fall, chunks of cement and roof screaming down like meteors, crashing to earth, diving into the water. And Hawker realized he should have waited until he was a hell of a lot farther away to detonate the damn thing.

He swung down into the icy water, taking the waves chest-high and losing his breath at first, as he waded toward shore. Twice, chunks of debris came way too damn close to hitting him, to killing him. Keeping one eye on the sky, the other on the rolling waves, he headed into shallow water, then immediately began to run.

Down the beach a ways he found it, the HEAT disposal missile and launching tube hidden in the bushes. Hawker slid out of his gear and lifted the thing, thinking once again that anything this light, this portable, shouldn't be trusted to do what it was intended to do.

But Hawker had used the HEAT before. He knew what it could do.

He snapped off the caps fore and aft, broke the plastic trigger guard, and touched the safety switch, arming the rocket.

Then he turned toward the rolling Chesapeake, squinting into the darkness. Where in the hell had the cruiser gotten to? He could no longer see it . . . could no longer see even the pale-white haze of its distant wake.

Hawker listened carefully—strained to listen, actually—while trying to ignore the steady wash and draw of waves. Then, for just a moment, he heard the faint grumble of engines carried on the cold wind, coming from somewhere southeast.

He leveled the launching tube, raised it slightly, then squeezed the trigger. There was a stunning *whoosh* as the rocket left the tube, throwing a snakelike trail of smoke and flame. It zigzagged crazily out to sea, gradually getting smaller and smaller until it disappeared altogether. And then there was nothing, only silence.

Hawker lowered the tube, perplexed. What the hell had happened? It was a heat-seeking missile, and the engines of the yacht certainly put out heat—

Thu-BOOM!

Far out on the horizon, maybe three miles away, there was a terrific explosion. The vigilante looked up in time to see the yacht illuminated in a corona of white light, its bow thrown high up out of the water, listing so far to starboard that, in that moment, he could see the whole top of the boat as if he were above it, and it would certainly roll over. Then there were only yellow flames, and he could see nothing else.

But the men aboard were dead—dead or dying, no doubt about that.

James Hawker picked up the caps of the spent rocket launcher and put them in the pack, which he now settled on his back. Then he walked quickly to his car, stored his gear in the trunk, and pulled onto the side road that would lead to the main road that would take him back to Norfolk. Driving carefully, relaxed now but shivering in the cold wool clothes, he did fifty miles an hour, just under the speed limit.

Hawker always obeyed traffic laws. Speeding was for pimply-faced teenagers and men-children who had never grown up and for adults who lived under the illusion that driving fast was, in some frustrated way, a method of expressing their virility. Speeding is just like anger, Hawker thought, getting pissed off and wanting to fight with absolutely nothing to be gained.

Anger was for amateurs.

James Hawker was no amateur.

six

HAWKER WAS BACK in his hotel room, a big two-room suite with a balcony that looked out over the cold, twinkling lights of Norfolk and the dark sea beyond. He took a long, hot shower, steaming up the whole bathroom. Then he wrapped a towel around his waist, feeling warm for the first time in about a year, it seemed.

He had gotten way too used to the sun and the heat and the balmy wind living down there on that stilthouse on the water in Everglades City, Florida. He had to toughen up, he knew that. It was way too easy down there in the land of sun and fun to end up a chubby, smiling beach bum, going through the female tourists and drinking margaritas.

Hawker got a bottle of beer from the refrigerator in the tiny kitchenette. Bud in a bottle. He stepped down into the sunken living room and studied the dial of the phone as he settled back onto a couch covered with oversized pillows. He asked the hotel operator to get him a number in Chicago. The bottle of beer was half empty when the operator rang him back, informing him that his party was on the line.

His party was Jacob Montgomery Hayes, his closest friend and multimillionaire associate who, when Hawker was first starting out as a vigilante, had provided financial backing and guidance. Now Hayes just provided guidance, using his staff and endless list of social and political connections to help Hawker in his work.

Hawker had his own money now, earned not through hard work but through blind luck. He paid his own way now.

Hayes seemed happy to hear from him, but his conversation was guarded, and he started off by saying "So how's the weather in your part of the country, James?" This was their standard code line, and meant that Hayes's electronic equipment was reading more than the normal amount of resistance on the phone line—meant, in other words, that someone was listening in or taping the conversation.

Who in the hell could it be? A nosy hotel operator? Cwong's organization? But how

could they already know who he was and
where he was staying? Or maybe the CIA—
that was the most likely possibility. Those boys
didn't let anyone stray far from their sight.

Hawker acknowledged Hayes's message by
answering "I don't know anything about the
weather, but the beer's cold," then continued,
"I met our friends a little earlier this evening."

Hayes was interested. "Oh? And how did it
go, James?"

"They seemed real surprised to see me."

"I'll bet. I hope they weren't too rude."

Hawker was smiling. "At first, maybe just a
little rude. But I did my best to settle them
down. You know me when I really turn on the
charm."

"A regular Valentino," Hayes said. "Will you
be going back to visit them again?"

"Really no reason to go back. I think we got
things pretty well straightened out."

"Oh?"

Hawker said, "I don't think our friends
would have another word to say to me. That's
how completely we went over that matter we
discussed. In fact, I don't think they'll have
much to say for a long time to come."

Now Hayes was smiling, Hawker could tell.
"Well, that *is* good news. Did the competition
show up?" Hayes meant the police.

Hawker said, "Not a sign of the competition.

In fact, I'm thinking about pulling out tomorrow. Not much more for me to do here."

"Fine," said Hayes. "Did I tell you our friends in Washington were trying to get in touch? They have a message for you."

"I'll give them a call," Hawker said.

"Great. They seem to be very worried about the lack of exercise you've been getting lately."

"About what?" Hawker wondered why his old friend was chuckling. What in the hell was he talking about?

"Your lack of exercise," Hayes repeated. "They're very concerned about that. But I'll let them tell you all about it. You remember the number, don't you?"

Hawker still couldn't figure out what was going on. He had expected Hayes to mention the name of a town where Hawker should strike Cwong's gang next. This business about exercise made no sense. He said, "Yeah, sure, I remember the number. I'll give them a call right now."

Jacob Montgomery Hayes was still chuckling as the vigilante hung up. Next Hawker called his CIA connection by private scrambler number; a few minutes later a message arrived by government courier, and he discovered why Hayes had been laughing.

The message read: *Upon completion of contractual work in Norfolk, please take the fast-*

est public conveyance to Coronado, California, to commence special SEAL training course.

Hawker sat back on the couch's plush cushions and finished his bottle of beer.

SEAL training.

That would get him back in shape, all right—if he survived it.

Not to mention get him ready to hit Cwong and Cwong's military stronghold on that island in the Solomons. . . .

Every morning they got him up at 4:30 A.M., had that damn bugler playing reveille over the PA system in the balmy California darkness, and then had that asshole CPO come charging through the barracks banging the garbage-can lid, telling them to get it done. "Piss, shit, and saddle up, boys." Just like in some John Wayne movie.

Hawker spent the first three days hating it and the next three too exhausted to even think. What in the hell was he doing out in the state of hot tubs taking orders from kids ten years younger than himself?

Getting in shape for the toughest mission of his career, that's what he was doing. He kept telling himself that's what it was all about as he willed himself through the hellish days of training. Every morning it was the same thing. He and seven other trainees—he guessed they were either CIA or maybe some special U.S. antiterrorist group; no one ever talked about why he was there—were herded into inflatable boats, where they shivered in the cold and dark as navy bosuns ran them two miles out into the sea before turning the boats eastward and pointing back toward the light haze of Coronado. "Enjoy your swim, sirs," the bastards would say. "Breakfast will be ready by the time you get back."

The first time it took Hawker and his group an hour and thirty minutes to get back, to come dragging their asses up onto the beach after fighting their way through the surf. The next day, though, they did it a little faster, then a little faster after that, and now, after eight days, they had their time down to under an hour, all of them swimming in formation.

But the morning swim wasn't the end of it—not by a long shot. After breakfast they did a warm-up jog of three miles. And if everyone didn't do it in under twenty-seven minutes, it was back onto the track for another quick mile. Then they did the obstacle course—the toughest damn obstacle course the vigilante had ever seen. It included a rope swing over jagged rocks as well as a white-water swim. Then it was lunch, and two hours of intensive hands-on explosives training—sometimes working underwater in the big dive tank.

After that it was back into running shoes, shorts, and navy sweatshirts, and onto the beach. "Got some telephone poles to move," the asshole CPO would holler happily. Then, in four-man teams, they'd grab a telephone pole, two men on each side, and do double-time a half mile down the beach, then switch hands and jog a half mile back.

The vigilante thought about quitting more than once, kept telling himself there was no reason to put himself through this crap. He told himself he had taken on tougher people than North Vietnam's Con Ye Cwong before and always had come out on top. He told himself he was wasting time, that every day he lingered, Cwong and his gang were getting stronger, growing richer, ruining more lives.

But he didn't quit. And for one reason, and one reason only. He had been ordered to Coronado by the organization that had retained him to destroy Cwong. And he didn't doubt that the CIA was right when his control officer insisted he needed more training to have a chance of taking Cwong's island. For another thing, the asshole CPO who woke him and the others up every morning clanging that damn garbage-can lid had just plain pissed him off. He seemed to look on Hawker and his group as a bunch of incompetent middle-aged suburbanites. Sneered at them. Laughed at them, like a man might laugh at a group of doddering old resthome cronies. And after the first three days when the hellish SEAL program made Hawker *feel* like some doddering old man, the vigilante decided he'd die before letting the navy CPO get the better of him.

After fifteen days of it—fifteen days of brutal physical and mental training, fifteen days of crawling into his Quonset hut bunk too tired to even talk, fifteen days of no beer but good navy food—Hawker stood looking in the mirror of the barracks head and saw that his face was lean from the weight he had lost—about eight pounds—and that his eyes no longer had that dull, sleepy South Florida beach bum look. Now they looked alive, lethally so. And his big hands were steady as rocks when he held them out.

He wasn't in the best shape of his life—but he was in the best shape he'd been in for maybe ten years. Plus he'd learned a few of the basic tricks of underwater demolition and had been brought up to date on some of the newest and most effective covert methods of operation.

Hawker was thinking all this as he stood looking at himself in the mirror of the empty barracks when, from behind, he heard the echo of rubber-soled shoes on the tile floor.

The vigilante turned to see Chief Stevenson,

the CPO who had been riding him and his group since their arrival in Coronado. Stevenson was maybe twenty-five, a lean, lanky young man who looked more like an Aspen ski instructor than the navy SEAL he was. Like Hawker, Stevenson wore the dark-blue cotton shorts and gray sweatshirt and field cap that was the PT uniform. The vigilante turned when he saw Stevenson, turned and smiled because he wasn't about to let the younger man know what an asshole he thought he was.

In return, he expected Stevenson to sneer. Stevenson had spent the last two weeks sneering at him, treating him like some raw eighteen-year-old boot. Stevenson was a good sneerer—he would bunch his big boney fingers into fists, shove the fists on his hips, crinkle his broad Marine Corps nose, push his head forward, and make a face like he smelled something bad.

Only now Stevenson didn't sneer. Instead he pushed his cap back on his head with a long index finger, smiled, and said, "Mr. Hawker?"

The vigilante tried not to show how surprised he was, but he couldn't help it. *Mr. Hawker.* Why was this kid suddenly being so polite?

Hawker said, "Am I late for something, Chief?" even though he knew he wasn't late for anything. It was chow time, and the vigilante had decided to skip lunch in order to get his weight down even more.

Stevenson was smiling now, looking oddly sheepish, almost shy. "You're not late for anything, Mr. Hawker," he said. "But the brass called me about fifteen minutes ago, said your training was through here. Said you'd be shipping out tonight. I just wanted to catch you before you got away and . . ." The big SEAL paused, not quite sure how to continue. Then he said, "I just wanted to apologize for being such a jerk."

The vigilante was still wearing the same mild smile, showing nothing. What in the hell was going on here? "Jerk? Not you, Chief. Why would I think you were a jerk?"

Stevenson said, "You kidding? I was riding you from the moment you arrived. But see, those were my orders—to get on your back and not get off. The big brass sent the orders, so I didn't have much choice, man. They wanted to make sure you stuck out the course, and they said getting you pissed at me was one sure way. Make you so pissed there was no way you'd drop out, let you think I'd run you out 'cause they said you were one man who'd never run. Ever. Said you'd hang on like grim death if I made it into a personal thing with you. Must be pretty important if they want you to stick with the program that bad, huh?"

Hawker shrugged, trying not to show how foolish he felt. He knew from where the orders had probably come. The suggestion to have some young CPO jump on his back had probably come from Jake Hayes himself, because Hayes knew him better than anyone else. Hayes knew Hawker worked best when there was some personal challenge involved. Hayes also knew how silly Hawker might feel having to go to boot camp after all he'd been through in the past three years.

Stevenson looked perplexed. "And you didn't even notice how hard I was getting on you, huh?"

"Guess I was too busy concentrating on the course to notice," Hawker replied.

"No kidding? Geez, I almost feel kind of bad about that. I was trying to be a real shithead. Just like those drill sergeants in the old movies, you know. Thought for sure I was getting to you, the way you looked at me sometimes. Kind of looked right through me, and, man—" The SEAL chuckled. "I don't mind telling you that you got a real scary way of looking at people. Made me feel like you were about an inch from going for my throat." Stevenson was shaking his head. "Anyway, Mr. Hawker, I just wanted to tell you that you are one tough old SOB. Some of the crap I put you through even made me flinch. And I've been in this business for seven, almost eight years now."

Hawker said, "I appreciate that, Chief. I really do. In fact, I'm kind of sorry it's over. I was just starting to enjoy getting back into shape."

"Yeah? Man, you're starting to make me feel real bad now. No one has ever left SEAL training, even a short course like this, saying he enjoyed it." Stevenson eyed him suspiciously. "What you got your weight down to? One eighty-five, maybe? Man, you look like you're getting into shape, huh?"

"Down to two oh two from two ten."

"No kidding, Mr. Hawker? I'd never guess you weighed that much. But yeah, now that I take a close look at your hands, your wrists, I see you probably weigh more than folks would guess. You're just full of surprises."

Hawker was smiling more broadly now. "I've got another surprise for you, Chief."

"Yeah? What's that?"

"I'm a terrible liar. You got to me the very first day I arrived here, and I've spent the last two weeks dreaming of ways to make you miserable after all this was over."

Stevenson looked genuinely pleased. "Hey, no kidding?"

"No kidding," answered the vigilante. "And I'll tell you something else. If I hadn't hated you so much, I probably would have split.

Probably would have left Coronado after the third day. Because you were, without a doubt, the nastiest, most thoughtless, toughest son of a bitch I've ever run into. And there was no way I was going to let such an asshole run me off."

Hawker had to laugh at the relief on the young CPO's face as Stevenson said, "Mr. Hawker, I appreciate that. I really do. You're not just saying that to make me feel better, are you?"

The vigilante took Stevenson's outstretched hand and shook it firmly as he said, "It's God's honest truth, Chief. I mean every word."

Stevenson said, "Mr. Hawker, coming from a guy like you, that means a lot. It really does. And if I can ever do anything else for you, please let me know. Hey, you going to be sticking around Coronado for a while? Maybe we could get together, hunt up some ladies and trade stories."

Hawker straightened his field cap in the mirror and said, "Naw, Chief, I'd like to. But after two weeks of you running my ass off, I think I'll take a little vacation."

Stevenson seemed interested. "You might try Carmel. They got some awfully pretty beach girls there."

Hawker said, "I was thinking of some place a little farther away. Like the Solomon Islands, maybe."

"The Solomon Islands? Yeah, sure, I guess that'd be pretty restful, huh?"

James Hawker said, "After SEAL training, it will probably seem like a picnic."

seven

___

THEY STUCK HIM on a military transport. Flew him from San Diego to Port Moresby, New Guinea, a hell of a long flight that followed the falling sun around the globe.

At the secret military installation outside Port Moresby, he was led to a Quonset hut on the far side of the camp and was met by three Americans dressed in plain gray suits.

No introductions were made. One man did most of the talking, a second man speaking up only when matters of geography were discussed. The third man, a Nordic-faced agent wearing dark Ray Ban sunglasses, never spoke at all. He just watched Hawker carefully, his expression flat, cold, emotionless.

The first man said, "We were very impressed

by the way you handled the assignment in Norfolk, Mr. Hawker.

Hawker just nodded. What was he supposed to say—thank you very much for telling me I'm good at killing people?

Motioning Hawker into a seat and then to a glass of iced tea on the desk beside him, the first man said, "So what do you think about New Guinea so far, Mr. Hawker?"

On the flight in, the vigilante had watched the wild forests and black rivers peel away beneath him. At one point he saw a group of dark men scurry off into hiding, as if frightened by the great steel bird. Once on the ground, though, he had seen nothing but the military PX and the base restrooms, which smelled of disinfectant. The base there looked just like the military base he'd left in San Diego, only a lot smaller. The vigilante said, "I'm looking forward to getting into the back country, having a look around. I hear some of the aboriginal tribes are still pretty much unspoiled by contact with the outside world."

The CIA agent said, "What?" as if not expecting anything but a mechanical answer. "Yes," he added, "that does sound interesting." And that was the end of the pleasantries. Getting down to work now, the agent said, "You have been briefed on General Con Ye Cwong's business operations?"

Hawker said, "A little. I know what he does, but I don't know how he does it—not that I really care. All I need is detailed data on his base of operations, help in getting there, and then I'll be happy to cut you and your men loose."

The man said, "I wish it were that easy, Mr. Hawker. I know that you're used to working alone, and I know you prefer to take the direct approach. I'm not saying you don't do your homework. If you weren't bright and accomplished, you wouldn't be here."

Hawker said, "Then what do you mean?"

The man said, "I mean that Cwong is not just some common crime boss. He's not anything like those mobs you dealt with in New York and L.A. Cwong is more like a . . ." The agent paused, seeking just the right words. "He's more like a king, a dictator. He demands—and receives—absolute loyalty from his people. To some of them the man is like a god. They look on him as one of the great leaders in the history of Vietnam—one of a handful of men who brought the United States of America to its knees. His people will fight to the death to protect him and his operation. And, as you can guess, Mr. Hawker, that kind of loyalty manufactures tremendous problems for people in our field to overcome."

Hawker said, "In other words, you have very

little specific data on Cwong because his people are so loyal they can't be bought. Or they're so terrified of Cwong, they're afraid to take the chance."

"See?" said the agent. "Your dossier says you're smart, Mr. Hawker. You catch on very quickly. And you're right—to a degree. But Cwong is involved in drug marketing in a big way. And I don't care how strict your rules about loyalty are—when you begin dealing with drug users you're vulnerable, because drug users have only one loyalty, and that's to their addiction. That's the big chink in Cwong's armor. We have detailed data on the way drugs are moved from his island to stations nearby and then put onto boats and planes for Hawaii and then the continental United States."

"But that still doesn't get me onto the island with Cwong," Hawker protested.

"It'll help. See, there are two major drop stations within twenty-five miles of Cwong's little paradise. And we've been able to compile plenty of data about both of them. We now know the exact expected time of drug shipments to both of the stations, how many boats are coming, and how many of Cwong's men are expected to be on the boats."

"So what?" said Hawker. "That still doesn't help me get next to Cwong. And that's what you want, isn't it? You want me to hunt down Cwong and kill him, right?"

All three CIA agents looked uncomfortable. The spokesman said, "Frankly, Mr. Hawker, we don't know the specifics of your orders. And we don't care. Our own orders say we're supposed to provide you with all possible assistance in getting you onto the island. That's the end of it."

"And what about helping me get *off* the island? Your orders don't say anything about *that?*"

Under the vigilante's steady gaze, the agents now appeared even more uncomfortable. Looking somber, the first man said, "We will, of course, help you off the island . . . if you survive. I hope no one gave you any illusions about this operation being easy. Because it won't be. Truth is, Mr. Hawker, I don't think anyone much expects you to come out alive. Like I said, Cwong is not your normal street thug. He's smart as hell and absolutely merciless." He looked at Hawker for a moment, then added, "You want me to continue with the briefing, Mr. Hawker? Or maybe you'd like to rethink your interest in the operation."

The vigilante gripped his iced tea in a steady hand and swallowed it in a single gulp. "I'm listening," he said.

* * *

The CIA agent stared intently at Hawker. "It's possible that choosing the night of one of Cwong's bigger deliveries will make it easier for you to slip onto his island unseen. His protection won't be at full strength. See, Mr. Hawker, Cwong has his own personal elite guards. Mostly upper-rank Viet Cong. They're absolutely ruthless. I think you'd have a better chance of succeeding on your mission if you caught Cwong while some of them were away from the island."

"That makes sense," said Hawker. "But how long will I have to wait?"

The agent shrugged. "According to our monitoring stations, two small deliveries are due in about four days. But nothing really big is coming up that we know about."

"You just want me to sit back and wait?"

"As I said, Mr. Hawker, our instructions are to assist you in any way we can. The final decisions as to where and how your strike will be are up to you."

"And you have almost no intelligence on Cwong's island? That makes for a pretty tough choice, gentlemen."

The first man nodded to the second, and the second agent pulled down a large wall chart showing the multitude of islands around the Solomons. The first agent said, "I didn't say that we had no intelligence on the island. I said we've been unable to get an insider to cooperate with us and feed us data. We have, of course, all the sophisticated machinery of intelligence gathering at our disposal. Through those means, we've compiled a fair amount of information on Cwong. We'll tell you what we know, what might be helpful, but, of course, we can't let you write any of it down. It's all highly sensitive material. It is, in fact, completely illegal for us to be involved with an operation like this at all. That's why we can offer you only limited assistance."

"I understand," said Hawker.

The second agent stepped forward, tapped the chart, and said, "Con Ye Cwong bought this island"—he touched a small, fluke-shaped island northwest of Guadalcanal—"ten years ago, not long after the fall of Saigon. Apparently others in the North Vietnamese army felt Cwong had grown too powerful. There was even a plot to have him assassinated. But they offered Cwong the option of leaving, and he jumped at the chance. Ended up in the South Pacific with about four hundred thousand in gold and U.S. currency and a handful of men. He began looking around for some remote estate to buy, and then he got wind of Kira-Kira, an island of about five thousand acres. Used to be an Australian settlement there, grew sheep, coconuts, pineapples, stuff like that. Hell of a thick jungle in the middle of the island. About fifteen years ago a couple of Japanese soldiers were discovered there, leftovers from World War II. Got blown off their ships and still weren't sure the war was really over. They were half crazy, of course, but it gives you some idea of what the interior of the island is like. Those men lived there unseen for thirty years, unnoticed, so far off the unbeaten path they had no inkling the war was over."

The vigilante was getting interested in the island, interested in Cwong as a person for the first time. He listened carefully.

The second agent said, "As you know, Cwong really has two main business operations going at the same time. One of those businesses is drug trafficking. That's how he made his fortune. Now he continues the business not just for profit, but out of genuine hatred for the American military. Truth is, we think he'd give the drugs away for free because he knows it's one of the surest methods of subversion available. A high percentage of military intelligence leaks have been traced directly or indirectly to drug dependence, and Cwong's organization is almost always at the root of it. But he's willing to trade drugs for something other than military secrets. He often trades for weaponry. American weaponry stolen by military personnel so they can keep their habits supplied, or so they can profit by selling the drugs to service people who are addicts. It's not just nickel-and-dime stuff, either. Five months ago ten gross of M-16s turned up missing from a military base on Guam. Not long after that an experimental Chrysler-made ATC full-track amphibian disappeared from the base at Honolulu—"

"They stole a *tank?*" Hawker asked incredulously.

"It's more than just a tank," the first agent cut in. "When we said experimental, we meant just that. This vehicle was capable of crossing five miles of heavy sea, driving up a rocky beach, ramming its way through thick jungle, and then attacking with either conventional ordnance or new laser weaponry. How in the hell they got it out, no one knows to this day. But a sting operation turned up an in-house drug ring that almost undoubtedly dealt with General Cwong. Cwong's become one of the world's leading armament and munitions dealers to outlaw groups around the world. He supplies any terrorist organization, so long as it has the money and so long as it's fighting the Western world. He's kind of like those stolen car dealers back in New York or L.A. A buyer tells Cwong what's needed, and Cwong's organization goes to work trying to steal it. He's got one hell of a big arsenal on that little island of his. And he blew a channel through the coral reef that surrounds the place so deep draft vessels can get in and out. But that channel is the only way to get in, so he has his own little fortress, like a separate country, really."

Hawker nodded. "What I don't understand," he said, "is why the United States just doesn't go in there under the guise of making some arrests, then use it as an excuse to blow the place apart. I mean, it sounds like you have enough proof."

The first agent said, "We'd like to. No, we'd *love* to. General Cwong has been a thorn in our side for too long. And if Kira-Kira was a U.S. or British protectorate, we'd take every legal means available to us to put him out of business. But it isn't. It's part of a small archipelago controlled by the French"—the agent cleared his throat uncomfortably—"and, if you know anything about the political workings of the French, you can understand why our hands are tied."

Hawker knew about the French. The French were, and had always been, the crybabies of the Western world. Politically they were forever getting themselves into trouble, and then they sat cowering in the corner while braver allies bailed them out—only to bite the hands of those same allies the moment the trouble was past. Personally the French people Hawker had known had been aloof, self-important snobs who seemed to go to great lengths not to bathe. On both levels, the French were first in only two areas: the first to cry for help and the first to refuse to help. He was not surprised the French had offered asylum to General Cwong. Fat bribes could smooth out nearly any wrong—including a hundred years of stormy French and Vietnamese history.

"So free-lancing is your only choice," Hawker said.

"Right," said the first agent. "And if you're linked to us in any way . . . well, let's just say it will be very unpleasant for all concerned."

Hawker almost said, *Which is why you'd prefer it if I didn't make it out alive,* but didn't. Instead he nodded to the charts and said, "Then let's get to work. I want every scrap of information you have. *Everything.* Everything from Cwong's muster power to his personal habits."

The second agent unrolled another bundle of charts while the third one lifted a large dossier file onto the table. The first agent said, "I think maybe we'd better send for some coffee, Mr. Hawker. We're going to be here for quite a spell."

eight

THE THREE AGENTS cut him loose around 10 P.M. They gave him a big brown envelope, which he opened after the government car deposited him on one of the back streets of Port Moresby, down by the wharfs. In it he found five thousand dollars in cash—twenties, fifties, and hundreds—all used bills. He folded the bills in four thick stacks, stuck one in each pocket of his khaki sea-worsted slacks, and buttoned the pockets shut.

Port Moresby was like every other tropical seaport town he'd been in. The buildings were dull, wind-blasted by the open ocean. The place smelled of diesel fuel and creosote and rust. The creaking cargo ships threw huge silhouettes against the South Pacific sky, and men walked in clusters through the narrow streets. Passing, Hawker caught snatches of strange languages: Arabic, Spanish, Japanese. One of those world crossroads, dingy and gaudy and filled with smells.

Hawker found the hotel the agents had recommended, the New Ireland, a tall old building with red carpet and a clunking elevator on pullies. Like a kid, the first thing he did when he entered his room was go into the bathroom, flush the toilet, and watch the water spin clockwise. Sure enough, he was on the underside of the globe, the place where everything works backward.

He thought about room service for dinner, then decided to go out. He showered, changed into a fresh Egyptian cotton shirt with epaulets, pulled on his felt planter's hat, put a hundred dollars in his pocket and a thousand in fifties and hundreds in his money belt, then put the rest, plus three thousand in cash of his own money, in an envelope and left it in the hotel safe.

He walked the streets for a while, almost stopping once at a Chinese restaurant and another time at a place that promised real Australian food—whatever that was—before spying a neon sign that read THE SAIGON: VIETNAMESE CUISINE.

Now, *that* might be interesting, thought Hawker.

The vigilante pulled open the door and saw a dimly lit room hazy with smoke. Pushing aside the beads, he stepped inside to the weird, discordant twangs and bongs of Asian music.

As his eyes adjusted, he saw a row of men hunched over their drinks at the bar, saw two sloe-eyed Asian women in tight silk skirts standing at the end of the bar, saw that half the tables were filled, with not a single Caucasian face in the place. He also noticed that the low buzz of conversation had halted as soon as he walked in, all eyes on the big dark-haired American with broad shoulders and Humphrey Bogart hat. That is, if they knew who Bogart was. He waited, wondering if one of the Asian women was a hostess. When neither of them made a move to show him to a table, he walked to the back of the room and sat down at one away from the wall, one where he'd have plenty of legroom. Still, neither of the women made a move toward him. He had the unmistakable impression that he wasn't exactly wanted at The Saigon and probably wouldn't get waited on—a fact that didn't bother him at all. As the Mormons said in those commercials, he'd turn the moment around.

Hawker stood, turned to the alleged hostesses, and said in a pleasant voice, "Excuse me.

I'd like to order dinner." The two women looked at each other, then at the tiny, wiry bartender. The bartender nodded. The youngest woman slid a menu off the bar with long red fingernails and came haughtily to Hawker's table, hips wagging, long black silken hair draped over one shoulder, and eyes burning. She dropped the menu in front of him and turned to go. "Wait a minute," Hawker said.

The woman stopped, looking over her shoulder at him.

"This thing is in Vietnamese. I don't read Vietnamese."

This elicited a big sigh from the waitress. "You come Vietnamese restaurant. What you expect?"

Hawker smiled. "Some help, maybe."

Another big sigh. "You eggspect me read whole thing? Read whole menu? Many things on menu. Maybe you better go some other place. You don't eggspect me read whole menu, do you?"

Hawker's smile broadened. "No. What I'd like you to do is choose something for me. You look like a woman who has good judgment when it comes to food. I'll put it in your hands. But first, a beer. Can you do that? A beer, then dinner."

A third sigh, only this one wasn't so big. She seemed to be softening some. "We have many beers," she said. "Many kinds. You want me tell you whole list? How I know what kind of beer okay?"

Hawker said, "Any kind of beer is okay. As long as it comes in a bottle and has bubbles, and as long as it isn't a beer called Pearl."

"Pearl?"

"Just bring me a beer in a bottle, no glass, then dinner. Okay? Like I said, I trust your judgment." Hawker was beaming at her, watching the haughtiness fade as she put a long fingernail to her lip, thinking. She said, "I give you nice traditional dinner. Okay? Nice dinner, plenty beer. That okay?"

"That's just fine," Hawker said. "I appreciate it." He watched the woman walk back to the bar, say something to the older woman, shrug at the bartender, say something else to the bartender, then put a tall liter bottle on a tray. She brought him the beer, hips wagging even more, small pointed breasts pressed flat by the tight dress. She set the beer on the table and watched Hawker look at the label he could not read. "You like?" she said. "Is okay?"

Hawker looked at the single big bubble that had formed at the neck of the bottle and at the label, which told him only that the beer had been bottled someplace in Cambodia. He looked at the waitress. "Good choice. It's one of my favorites."

The woman seemed pleased. "So I bring you dinner now?"

"You bring me dinner now. Right."

When she had gone, Hawker tasted the beer tentatively. Then again. It was excellent, one of the best beers he'd ever had. It reminded him of Hatuey, the Cuban beer the Baccardi family had bottled before Castro ran them out. He drank the beer, still aware that his every move was being watched, aware that the whole room was uncomfortable with him there but still not minding it at all, wanting to see how the men in the room reacted to him. He was sure that many of them were linked in some way to General Con Ye Cwong. Had to be, this close to Kira-Kira. In all the faraway places of the world, people of the same race stuck together.

Then the dinner came. It was not as good as the beer. Some kind of curry with meat and gravy over rice, plus side dishes of nearly raw vegetables, tomatoes and bean sprouts and something else Hawker couldn't identify. A lot of gray rice. He ate it all because he was hungry. He was surprised when the waitress, whose name was Sha Hainan, actually stopped to make conversation. She asked him where he was from, what he was doing in New Guinea. He told her he was an American investor interested in pineapple and coconut plantations. She accepted it without question. When he caught her glancing at his left hand, looking for a wedding ring, he knew that he had ceased to be just a big ugly American, had in fact become a monied person whom she was interested in. Hawker decided to try something, just to see how she reacted. "There's an island in this area I heard about," he said. "A place called . . . Kira-Kira? Something like that. Heard there used to be a big plantation there. You know if it might be for sale?" He watched as her expression changed; he saw that guarded look.

"Kira-Kira? Yes, I know. No, no for sale. Sure of that."

Hawker pressed on, aware that people nearby were listening more closely now. "They still grow pineapples there? I heard some Aussies used to have it, had a hell of a big grove there. It sounds like just the kind of place I'm looking for."

"No," she said quickly. "Don't know who own it."

"Then how do you know it's not for sale?" Hawker asked.

"Just know, that's all. Just know. Hey, you want more beer? Dessert maybe?" Hurrying him along now, already placing the check on the table, she turned away, ending the conversation.

Hawker stood, put his hat on, saw that the bill was padded, way too much, but left a ten on the table as a tip anyway. Sha Hainan knew something about Kira-Kira, that was clear. If his stay on New Guinea was lengthy enough, maybe he could work it out of her later.

Headed for the cash register, he tripped unexpectedly. Catching his balance before he fell, Hawker looked back to see that a man had stuck his foot out. Now the four other men, all Vietnamese, were laughing into their hands, looking up at him.

Hawker walked to the table and stood over the man who had tripped him. A chunky, squat Vietnamese man, with long black hair, greased and combed back. Hawker said, "Friend, you didn't do that on purpose, did you?"

The laughter slowed, then stopped. The man looked up at Hawker with no fear at all in his eyes and said, "Got to watch where you're walking, man. You go plodding along, no watch. Got to watch out, you maybe take a bad fall, huh?"

Hawker moved a little closer, making the Asian crane to look at him. He said, "See, the problem is, if someone tried something childish like that on me, tried to trip me for no reason, I'd have a real urge to beat the hell out of him. You understand?"

The man was still looking up, leaning back. "Hey, man, don't give me no hard time, huh? You clumsy, you trip, coulda hurt somebody.

Coulda spilled all our drinks. Maybe make us want to beat the hell out of you, huh? Maybe you shouldn't come to places you not wanted. Real easy for a guy like you to trip in a place like this."

Hawker looked around and saw that every man in the place was sitting closer to the edge of his seat, ready to stand and take part if it went any further. Hawker nodded, then smiled. "Well, maybe you're right. Maybe I should be more careful." He saw that look in the eyes of the men at the table, that glittering dog-fight look of the victor when the weaker animal begins to retreat.

The chunky Vietnamese said, "See, you catch on quick for a Yankee. Most you too dumb to catch on. Have to beat the hell out of you, you no catch on."

The room was buzzing now, the men laughing as Hawker walked to the bar to pay the padded bill. Just loud enough for everyone to hear, the chunky man said, "They cowards, man, see? Big Americans all cowards."

Hawker jammed the change in his pocket. He looked at Sha, and she quickly turned away, ashamed for him, not wanting to be associated with this humiliated American. After crossing the room in three long steps, he stopped by the table again, towering over the chunky Vietnamese. The Asian men stopped laughing, wondering why the American was grinning at them. They watched as the American picked up a full glass from the table, and, holding it to the light, said, "What's this crap you're drinking?"

"Hey, man, put that down, huh," said the fat Vietnamese man. "You no wanted here, Mr. Amer—" The man started to get to his feet, but the vigilante clamped a big hand on his shoulder, forcing him back into his chair.

"I'd like to buy you a fresh drink for all the trouble I caused. You don't mind, do you?"

Wincing under Hawker's grip, the man said, "No, buy me drink. Fine. Then get the hell out, huh?"

"Good. But I better empty this glass first." Hawker poured the black liquor and ice over the man's head. "There. Now you're ready for a fresh drink."

All hell broke loose then as the chunky Vietnamese swung at Hawker, hitting him right above the belt, just missing the groin. The vigilante didn't give him a chance to try again. He hit the man flush in the neck with a solid right cross, then split his nose open with another right that knocked the man out of his chair, unconscious and bleeding on the floor.

At this point someone tried to jump on Hawker's back from behind, and he ducked down, hitting his head painfully on the table. He

swung back with his elbow, felt it connect sol-
idly, and heard a grunt of pain. Next he turned
and dropped another man with a glancing left
fist to the throat, as the bartender came over
the bar swinging a baseball bat. Hawker caught
the bat on the backswing, kicked the little bartender's feet out from under him, then used
the knob of the bat to shatter the teeth of a
man who charged him from across the room.

Women were screaming, men cursing as
they tried to circle him. The vigilante knew
that if he let them get too close, if he let them
get him on the floor, he was a dead man. Someone lifted a beer bottle, and Hawker hit it with
the bat instinctively, shattering glass and beer
all over the place.

Hawker kept his back to the bar. He glanced
over his shoulder to see what kind of gauntlet
he had to run to get to the door. Three wiry
men stood blocking his path, brandishing broken bottles. Getting out was not going to be
easy, and it was not going to be pretty. He
began to edge his way along the bar, fending
off attackers with the bat. Someone hit him
from the side, pinning his arms, trying to wres-
tle him to the floor. Hawker got the man's foot
under his own, locking him in place, and finally
kicked him hard between the legs with his
knee. As the man slumped away yowling, the

vigilante turned back just in time to crack open the face of another man with his big left fist.

The screaming and swearing had become more subdued now, if that was possible, leaving a brutal whoofing and grunting sound that sounded like some kind of primitive prayer. A half-dozen men lay groaning or unconscious on the floor, and the rest were working their way around him, trying to surround him.

Hawker paused; he looked around, trying to figure out a better way to exit. Suddenly he caught the cat eyes of Sha, the Asian waitress, and saw her nod ever so slightly to a doorway behind the bar. The vigilante did his best imitation of a karate yell and lunged at the men coming slowly at him. As they jumped back in momentary terror, he vaulted over the bar, got to the doorway, and saw that it led outside to an open alley. He stopped in the doorway, just for a second, smiled and gave a brief salute. "Enjoyed it!" he called. "Let's do it again real soon."

Hawker sprinted down the alley and out into the main street, losing himself in the midnight pedestrian traffic, walking easily now, hardly out of breath at all after his ass-kicking stay with the Coronado SEALs.

Hawker studied his bruises and swelling knuckles under the glare of a streetlight. Nothing seemed to be broken. He touched the

tender spot on his forehead where he had hit
the table—and realized something else.

James Hawker swore softly beneath his
breath.

He'd gone off and left his hat at The Saigon.

Maybe he'd go back and get it . . . some
other time.

nine

BACK AT THE hotel, Hawker discovered he had left not only his hat at the restaurant; he had lost his room key too. What's next? he wondered as he approached the front desk clerk for a duplicate.

Once inside his room, he ordered a bucket of ice, beer, and aspirin from room service. He tried to pronounce the name of the Cambodian beer but couldn't. He took a shower while he waited for his order, soaking his body. Then he flushed the toilet a couple of more times, just to watch the water spin. He dressed himself in a T-shirt, soft running shorts, and Nikes. When room service arrived, Hawker tipped the boy, a kid who looked like a pure-blooded aborigine, then took the aspirin, made an ice pack to wrap around his knuckles, and drank the beer while he spread out the charts from the envelope the CIA men had given him.

The island of Kira-Kira lay about three hundred miles to the northeast, a green link in the long chain of islands that formed the Solomons. Immediately to the east of Kira-Kira, closer to Hawaii, were two smaller islands, Tongo and Mokii, which the agents had said were Cwong's two main drop stations.

Hawker found the detailed charts that showed each island separately in minute detail. The charts showed the sharp volcanic ranges and indicated beaches, reefs, man-made structures, and dense jungle. He paid special attention to aerial photos of Kira-Kira. Hawker could see clearly a huge house at the center of a compound fenced by stone; he could pick out guard towers and outbuildings; he could clearly see the hole Cwong had blasted through the reef and the deep narrow channel that led to the huge industrial-size wharf, complete with crane. The big landing strip and the stretch of jungle that the agents had said was actually a camouflaged area where Cwong stored his armaments were clearly visible on the map.

The place looked damn near invincible—except maybe for one thing: Cwong's fortress was backed against a jagged volcanic outcropping, like a small mountain. That, of course, would be the most likely place from which to approach, because Cwong would know there was no way a large body of men could be marched down it.

Which was the main advantage of working alone. Alone, he could make it. Maybe.

The vigilante pored over the charts, memorizing the details one by one. He gave close attention to a tiny unnamed island seven nautical miles from Kira-Kira, which the CIA agents said would be an ideal departure point for him. It had been agreed they would cache any requested weaponry there, complete with an Avon inflatable and a seventy-horse-power outboard—a real screamer.

Hawker finished reviewing the charts as he finished his second beer. Then he urinated, stripped, switched on the lamp beside the bed, and lay down to watch a Vietnamese-speaking television station before sleeping. He knew he wouldn't understand a word of it, but also knew that the noise and moving images would soon make him drowsy.

It was 1:35 A.M.

He watched a young Vietnamese woman in a flowing silk robe dance exotically and sing incomprehensibly for about half an hour before hearing a sound outside his door. The whispered creak of footsteps. Then the sound of metal touching the lock on his door.

The vigilante was on his feet in an instant, the chrome-plated Smith & Wesson .45 heavy in his hand. He moved silently across the floor, stopping beside the door with his back to the wall. The handgun felt cool alongside his face as he waited.

Hawker watched the doorknob turn, saw the door crack open. The vigilante grabbed the wrist that held the knob and jammed the barrel of the automatic against the temple of . . . of Sha Hainan, the waitress from the restaurant.

She gasped, trembling beneath his grip. Her small, delicate voice cried out, "No hurt, please. No hurt me. I brought you something."

Hawker swung the woman into the room way too hard, the adrenaline pumping through him. Kicking the door closed with his foot, he said, "You could have knocked, for Christ's sake! You trying to get yourself killed?"

The woman, who had pulled away from him, stood cowering against the wall, crying. She was still wearing the tight red dress, looking tiny and frightened.

Hawker took a deep breath and lowered the .45. "Hey," he said. "I'm sorry. I'm sorry I was so rough on you. But I had no idea it was you. I knew I'd lost my key, probably during the fight, and I thought maybe some of those guys had come to even the score—" Then he saw what the woman held in her left hand. "You found my hat," he said, smiling.

For some reason, the woman refused to look at him. Then he realized why: He was completely naked.

He walked to the table, pulled on his running shorts, and said, "There. Is that better?"

The woman stepped away from the wall, holding out the gray felt hat. "I sorry I frightened you. No wrong meaning. Just wanted to bring you hat, key. Reason I didn't knock was because . . . because . . ." She looked at the floor. "Someone might hear. Someone might see me come, get wrong idea. In this town, all women look like me considered whore. This a small-town place. My reputation good."

Hawker wondered why she didn't just leave them at the desk, but didn't press it. "And your reputation will stay good, Sha. I appreciate your coming." He reached out, took the hat, creased it, tried it on, winced as the hat band settled on the bump that had formed on his forehead.

Sha pressed her fingers to her lips, shielding a giggle. "You look funny in hat. Very funny, hat, not shirt or shoes."

Hawker raised his eyebrows. "I'm lucky to be here at all after that little party your friends threw for me back there at the restaurant. They always treat Americans that way?"

The smile left her catlike Asian face. "They no my friends. They mean to everyone, those people. All bad. You hurt many of them. Three go to hospital. They very mad at you there. Looking for you, they say."

"But you helped me," Hawker said. "Why?"

Sha sat in the chair across from him as the vigilante took a seat on the bed, saying "Don't know why. In restaurant, you seem nice. No pushy. No bossy. Leave everything up to me. That man trip you. I see it. Very frightened they hurt you."

"And that's why you came here? Just to bring me my hat and tell me you were frightened I would be hurt?"

Sha shook her head slowly. "No, that not the only reason I come. I come tell you not to ask about Kira-Kira. Very important I tell you something."

"Oh?"

"Yes. Kira-Kira a bad thing to say here. Very dangerous. Do not mention it around my people. Make them very nervous. Make them very mean."

"They have something against the island?" Hawker asked, playing innocent. "I don't understand."

"Don't need to understand. Just understand

Kira-Kira a very bad place. Very bad. Never ask
no more. Never ever try to go there. Bad
things happen to you, you try."

"You've been there, then? You've been to the
island?"

In a small voice Sha said, "As a girl I live
there for two, maybe three years. My father
work there for . . . for man owns it."

"Does he still live there?"

"No," she said. "He dead. Man who own island kill him. Murder him for no reason. Murder him 'cause my father a fair man. No like
things happening on Kira-Kira. Take him out
one night and he never come back. I no have
mother, she killed in war by Viet Cong. Man
come tell me my father fall off boat, drown. I
no believe him, even as young girl. I know my
father a swimmer, very good swimmer. No
way he drown. Man who own island want me
to come be his little daughter. But that lie too.
Really want to do things to me. Bad things—"
She shuddered, unable to speak for a moment.

Hawker went to her, touching her gently on
the arm. "It's okay," he said. "You don't have to
talk about it if you don't want."

Sha lifted her head, looking carefully into the
vigilante's eyes. "I no mind. Am very proud of
it. Very proud of how strong I was, just little girl
all alone. I escape. Ten year old, and I find
secret way off island. I escape, and man who

own island don't even care enough to find out I live or die. I come here, live with nuns till I go out on my own. Only place hire me was The Saigon. Now I save money to leave this place. Someday. Leave these bad people of mine. Someday go to United States where things are fair. Get my freedom there."

"But this bad man who owns Kira-Kira certainly knows that you work at the restaurant. The Vietnamese community here isn't that large."

"Yes, he know. But he no bother me. No longer interested. No longer a little girl. See, I a woman now. This man not like womens, only girls."

"Then he is a very bad man indeed," Hawker said.

"Yes. Oh, yes. Very bad. That why you must not ask questions about pineapples and coconuts. You want grow the fruits, many islands around very good for that. But you ask questions about Kira-Kira, my people get wrong idea. Think you maybe here to bother the bad man on his island. They protect him. They all protect him."

Hawker thought for a moment. "How much money do you need to save before you think you can leave for America, Sha?"

The woman shrugged. "Don't know exactly. Have saved six hundred dollars on my own.

Got it in bank, save a little every day. You are American. How much more you think I need?"

"You'll need a lot more than that, Sha—unless you want to get there and immediately be broke. End up the same way you're living here. I'd say you need several thousand. Enough to stake you for a few months while you find a decent job." Hawker smiled. "Hey, don't look so discouraged. I think I know a way for you to make all the money you need."

Sha, looking suspicious, said, "Men in restaurant tell me that, offer me much money. I know what they want." She touched her knee. "I keep knife to protect myself. I like you, but no try something. I no like men that way."

"No man at all, Sha?"

"No," she said in a husky voice.

"Never?"

"Never." She turned and looked at him. "You are first man I see without clothes. First American man, anyway. When I was little girl, I saw that man owns Kira-Kira. It true what they say. Very true."

"And what do they say, Sha?"

Her face colored. "American men very big. Very large. Too large. Not enough money to make me do that."

"And I wouldn't offer you money for that, Sha. But I'd like to hire you to do something else."

"No drugs," she said, still distrustful of Hawker. "I no carry drugs. I a decent girl. Say the rosary every day, pray to God to help me get to America. Go to mass, go to confession too."

Hawker wondered what she had to confess. "I don't want to hire you to carry drugs, Sha. It's something else. You said you found a secret way out of Kira-Kira when you were a little girl. Do you think you could still find it, that secret way? I'd pay you a lot of money to show it to me. Enough money to get you to America and support you there for several months."

The woman stood, an expression of wonder on her face. "You no hear what I tell you? You no believe what I say? You go Kira-Kira, they kill you! Many men there. Many soldiers, much guns! They see you, big strong American, they not even ask your name, just go boom-boom, good-bye, mister. Why you must grow pineapples on that place? Many other islands to buy. Many better places, not so much jungle—" Then her expression began to change, from outrage to slow understanding as she met the vigilante's cold gray eyes. "Wait a minute . . . *you* no planter. You say you want grow coconuts, pineapples, but you lying to me. You come here for other reason, no? You come here spy on General Cwong, man who own Kira-

Kira. Tell me truth now. That the reason you come."

Hawker decided to follow his instincts. He felt the story Sha Hainan had told him was true, although he would certainly check out what he could about her later. But if he was to make a deal with her, he would have to make it now, before she had a chance to rethink it, to consider the danger involved. Besides, finding some secret trail through the jungles of Kira-Kira was worth the risk. He said, "I didn't come here to spy on Con Ye Cwong, Sha."

"Then why you must go that island? If you a planter—"

"I'm not a planter or an investor either. I came to kill Cwong. I came to kill him and destroy as much of his operation as I can. And I would like to pay you to help me."

The woman sat down again, eyeing him steadily, breathing through her nose. She studied her hands for a moment, then looked up. "You come kill Cwong?"

"Yes, Sha, that's right."

"Then I help you. Help you any way I can. Only you no need pay me. I help because I want."

"If you want to think it over for a while—"

"Already thought it over," she cut in. "Thought it over many times. Thousands times. Cwong killed my father, did bad things to me." She looked at him then, her dark feline eyes glowing. "For many years I knew you would come. I waited and waited and finally give up."

"You knew I was coming?" Hawker asked.

"Yes," the woman said. "Because living with the nuns I ask for you. Many years I ask for you. I pray for man to come help me kill Cwong. . . ."

ten

HAWKER SPENT THREE long days in Port Moresby, waiting.

He hated waiting, despised inactivity.

And so he found himself doing calisthenics every morning and taking long runs through the city every day. Sailors looked at him as if he were some crazy tourist, shaking their heads. But he kept it up every day, not wanting the fine physical edge honed at Coronado to wear off.

After exercising, he'd return to the hotel and study the charts, memorizing every last detail.

The CIA didn't expect him to come out alive. Sha didn't expect him to come out alive. Well, he wanted to prove them wrong. He liked surprising people, being an underdog—but one who emerges victorious.

Most of all, though, he wanted to surprise Cwong.

In the past few weeks, a picture of Con Ye Cwong had gathered detail in his mind, like an image on photographic paper coming to life in a tub of chemicals. Dull gray at first, the image soon took on details, shades of light and black, and finally came into sharp focus, to life.

Cwong was alive in Hawker's mind now, a living, breathing creature, a fat spider comfortable in his web.

On one level, Cwong was a zealot motivated by greed and hatred. He liked money, he loved power, he hated Americans. A political animal who thought nothing of murder. On another level, Cwong was one of the twisted ones, one of those brain-damaged predators who feed on the human spirit, who draw strength from destroying those unfortunate enough to fall under their power. If he couldn't kill them, he got them hooked on drugs and destroyed them that way. Or he provided weaponry to other zealots. On a third level, certainly his most personal and repulsive level, Cwong was an abuser. Not of women. Women were strong. Too strong. So he went for children. Girl children, certainly. Maybe boy children too.

Cwong took them when they were too weak to fight back.

Hawker had a clear picture of the man, all right. A killer. A destroyer. A rogue animal filled with disease.

This might be his toughest assignment, but he had never come to an assignment with greater resolve.

Hawker wanted this man. He wanted to look him in the eye and tell the bastard why he was being killed before pulling the trigger.

For once Hawker's role wasn't that of a vigilante. He was now an executioner, plain and simple.

And James Hawker had come across few men more deserving of an executioner.

So he waited for three days, itchy as hell, anxious to do what he did best. He had told Sha that they must not meet again, must not see each other or be seen together before it was time to leave. Her people would certainly kill her if they found out she was involved with him in any way.

She had agreed without question, trusting him totally because, after all, he had been sent as an answer to her prayers. When he needed to get in touch with her, she said, he could stop at the convent outside town. The nuns would get in touch with her, give her any message.

Without her knowledge, and with the help of

military intelligence at the Port Moresby base, Hawker had found out her bank, her account number, and had deposited five thousand dollars in her name.

Then, in the morning of the fourth day, Hawker went out for his usual long run. He had stopped outside the hotel door, deciding which way to go, when a man leaning against the building in a gray suit said in a low voice, "You're not going to have time to go for your run, Mr. Hawker."

The vigilante stopped. He looked at the man, then looked away. With all the people passing by, he decided just to listen. The voice said, "At noon you will go to the public docks on Three Britain Street and charter a boat called *The Blue Marlin*. Ask for Captain Watson. Can you hear me?"

Hawker nodded.

"Good," the voice said. "Ask for Captain Watson, and tell him you want to fish for anything that will bite. Got that? Anything that will bite. Carry your personal gear along, everything you might need for a long stay. *The Blue Marlin* will take you to an island about forty miles from here. Just after dusk a chopper will land, then take you to a place near your assignment. The pilot will tell you where to find your boat. You will take that boat to the unnamed island not far from Kira-Kira. The pilot will also tell you where to find your equipment and where the best place to stay on that island is. Our friend on Kira-Kira will be making deliveries two days from today, on Thursday, probably around midnight. Nod if you have it all."

Hawker said, "I have it all. But tell Captain Watson there will be two of us."

The voice became strident. "No. No way. Just you—"

"That wasn't a request," Hawker interrupted. "There will be two of us." Hawker looked at the man. "Nod if you understand."

The man in the gray suit looked confused for a moment, then finally nodded.

"Good," said Hawker. "I'm going for my run."

Hawker ran past the city limits signs to the convent, old and made of brown rock. He shook the big brass knob until a tiny nun answered, and told her he had an important message for Sha. The nun nodded as if she had been expecting him, then produced paper and pencil from somewhere in her habit.

Hawker wrote a brief note, dated it, folded it, handed it back to the nun, and said, "Sha has to see this within the hour. I can take it if you tell me where she is."

The nun stuffed the note away. "It will be

taken care of." She backed into the compound, closing the big door.

Hawker turned back for town, running hard, pushing himself, feeling the sweat pour out. He stopped at the hotel's front desk and told the clerk he was going on a fishing trip but wanted to keep his room. Might not be back for a day or two, he explained, but wanted to pay for a week in advance, just to set your minds at rest.

He went up to his room, showered, dressed in fresh cotton slacks and navy-blue shirt, packed his stuff, then drew five hundred from the hotel safe, just in case.

Walking down the street toward the wharf at Three Britain Street, Hawker felt strong, healthy, and alive, ready to take on Cwong.

He could almost smell the man, that's how close he felt. It wasn't a pleasant smell, that much was for sure.

The Blue Marlin was a forty-two-foot Bertram, dark-blue hull, white superstructure, name in big gold letters across the transom and landing gate. There were outriggers and a flybridge, plus a comfortable cabin with bunks.

Captain Watson was a short, thick man, with big shoulders, big hands, and an equally big British accent. A varnished tan testified to many years spent on these dark-blue waters. Hawker guessed he was a real captain, and

probably an occasional employee of the CIA as
well. Watson, who was sitting in one of the
plush fighting chairs when Hawker came stroll-
ing down the dock, looked up at the vigilante
sleepily from beneath the bill of a Greek fisher-
man's cap.

"You open for charter?" Hawker called to
him. Other men in nearby boats looked up,
listening.

Watson pushed the bill of the cap up with his
index finger. "Maybe. What you got in mind?
You want to fish for blues?"

Hawker remembered the code phrase. "I
want to fish for anything that'll bite."

Watson stood up, waving. "Come on aboard
then. We'll discuss price."

Hawker carried his gear on board. Watson
took him below, showed him where to store his
stuff, and gave him a can of iced tea. He said, "I
hear you're expecting a friend, Mr. Hawker."

Hawker nodded. "A woman. She used to live
on Kira-Kira. Having a guide might be a big
help."

Watson smiled. "I hope she's beautiful.
You're going to end up on a tiny little island
that doesn't have a goddamn thing on it but
trees and monkeys and beach. Two days there
are going to seem like two weeks—unless you
have something to entertain you."

Hawker didn't smile. "It's not that kind of relationship."

Watson, visibly disappointed, went back to the fighting deck to wait for Sha. The vigilante watched through the oblong portholes, not wanting to spend too much time outside, out in the open.

He saw a nun coming down the pier. Her head was bowed, her hands hidden within her sleeves. She was walking rather fast. Hawker felt a surge of disappointment, knowing the nun was probably coming to tell him Sha had changed her mind about coming. He raced the three steps to the fighting deck and said, "Sister?"

Standing on the pier at the stern of the boat, the nun looked up and smiled.

It was she. It was Sha.

Watson looked at Hawker. "That's her? The woman we're waiting on?"

"That's right."

Watson grimaced. "Geez, Mr. Hawker, I'm sorry about that crack I made a little bit ago. I had no idea—"

"Save it for confessional, skipper." Turning to Sha, Hawker said, "Can we drop you somewhere, Sister?"

Sha didn't answer, but hiked her skirt up just enough to step on board, the veil she wore not dark enough to obscure her lovely face. She carried a small carpetbag with her, and the vigilante took it. "You'll probably want to go below where it's cooler, Sister. We have a long ride ahead of us."

She went down the steps without comment.

Hawker helped Watson with the lines, and soon *The Blue Marlin* idled out of the harbor, taking it slow through the short no-wake zone. Standing on the flybridge with Watson, Hawker could see the white surf at the mouth of the inlet. Watson pressed the throttles and the big twin turbo-charged diesels growled as the boat gained speed, its bow riding high and throwing white sheets of water to each side of the vessel. And then *The Blue Marlin* plunged out into the glittering expanse of blue open sea.

Watson dropped some teaser baits back and loaded the outriggers, the lines baited with big iridescent konas. He said they had to play the game at least until they were out of sight in case some other vessel was keeping an eye on them.

The vigilante saw no other vessels, but didn't mind the captain's precautions. It was pleasant sitting in the big fighting chair, feet up, trolling along over the long greasy rollers of the South Pacific. Twice the outriggers snapped, and Hawker reeled in big mahimahi, the beautiful gold-and-turquoise fish he knew back in Florida as dolphin.

He released both of them, then reset the outriggers.

Sha reappeared after half an hour, still wearing the habit. She held onto the fighting chair, standing over Hawker's shoulder, then looked up to see if Watson could hear. Satisfied he couldn't, she said in a soft voice, "He taking us to Kira-Kira? It a very long way by boat, you know."

"I know. But he's taking us to a place where we'll meet a helicopter. The helicopter is going to take us to another island, one not far from Kira-Kira. We may have to stay on that island alone for a few days. You don't mind, do you?"

"I no mind. But very hot in this clothes." She adjusted her veil uncomfortably. "You must be saint to wear this."

"Was it your idea to dress like that?"

"No. Sister Mary Margaret's idea. Sister Mary Margaret very smart. Much trust for her, so I tell her what I do. No tell her we kill Cwong, that a mortal sin and she could not help. Just tell her we go spy, maybe help police stop him. She know what bad man he is. She worry for me, ask me to dress like this. A good idea, no?"

"A good idea, yes—" Something had caught Hawker's attention. Behind the skittering teaser bait fifty yards behind the boat, he saw the huge black fin and scimitar tail of a marlin.

The fish was trailing the big artificial lure, its great bill swinging back and forth, knocking at it.

Despite the seriousness of the mission they were on, it was still a thrilling sight. He yelled up to the flybridge. "Hey, Watson! Look at the size of that thing!"

The charterboat captain glanced back, then did a double take. "Holy shit, reel in quick before he hits it—" Watson looked quickly at Sha, his face crimson. " 'Scuse my language please, Sister, but that is one goddamn big fish!"

It really was a big fish. Hawker yanked the rod out of the holder, shoved the fighting drag forward on the Penn International Gold reel, snapped the line out of the outrigger clip, and began to reel furiously, trying to keep the fish away from the bait. He was sorry as hell they didn't have time to try to catch it.

But reeling only seemed to enrage the fish, and the marlin surged after it, chasing the bait with great sweeping strokes of its tail, its fin up higher now, its body glowing a molten, iridescent blue. It suddenly dawned on Hawker that if he kept reeling, the fish might collide with the boat. That's how determined the marlin was in its pursuit.

He stopped reeling abruptly and the bait began to sink. The fish sounded, and then Hawker felt a tremendous impact, the rod bowing with a weight greater than he had ever felt, jerking him sideways onto the deck.

The reel was screaming now as the fish ran, and Hawker looked up from the deck just in time to see the fish come out of the water. The neon-bright creature was massive. It looked as big as a car, its great head shaking as if in slow motion, its whole body sweeping this way and that like a dancer in midleap, throwing quarts of water that glittered in the sun like opals.

Then it crashed back into the sea with a tremendous splash, and slow-motion time was over, everything after that happening at tremendous speed.

"That fucking thing must weigh fifteen hundred pounds!" Watson yelled from above, then immediately looked at Sha again for forgiveness.

"Fifteen hundred, hell," she answered, unfazed. "Big bastard must weigh whole ton!"

The surprise on Watson's face turned to pleasure. "Goddamn right, Sister! A fucking ton!"

Watson had locked both engines in neutral, and Hawker knew how tempted he must be to try to regain some line and catch the thing. The fish continued to run at an astounding rate, then jumped again, still looking huge even two football-field lengths away.

When the fish dropped back into the sea, the vigilante pointed the rod tip directly in its direction, braced himself against the transom, then shoved the drag lever beyond the little safety ball bearing, locking the spool.

There was a stunning jolt, and then nothing.

The vigilante reeled the line in, studying it where it had broken above the Bimini twist that had been tied to the swivel and leader. He looked up and saw how disappointed Watson was. "You tie good knots, Captain Watson," he said. "Line broke exactly where it should have."

"That was the fish of a lifetime," Watson allowed. "The fish of a damn lifetime. I've never seen a bigger marlin in my life. Never. And I've seen a lot of them." He shook his head miserably. "The bloody damn things I go through for the bloody damn good of the cause —'scuse me again, Sister."

Hawker wondered what cause Watson was talking about but didn't ask. Instead he said, "Maybe when all this is over, we'll go fishing again. He's still out there. That hook will corrode out in a couple of days, and he'll be ready to feed again."

But all Watson would say as he pushed the boat up to full throttle was, "Not that fish, Mr. Hawker. Not that fish. A man only gets a chance at a fish like that once in a lifetime."

Hawker sat back in the fighting chair, his heart still pounding. The woman pressed her

hand on his shoulder, patting him. "I glad," she
said softly. "I glad he get away. Big fish deserve
freedom too. . . ."

An island lifted out of the sea, lifted and fell
with the rhythm of the waves.

Then Hawker could see a single cement
wharf loaded with oil drums and a shack with a
tin roof beyond the white beach.

He was back on the flybridge with Watson
now. Sha was below, resting.

"That's it, Mr. Hawker. There's the island
where the chopper will pick you up. Doesn't
look like it's there yet, but we made a little
better time then I thought we would. Even
with the fish, it only took us two and a half
hours. Good sea today."

"I meant that about fishing again when I'm
done with this," Hawker said. "I'd like to take
an honest shot at a big blue."

"You make it back, Mr. Hawker, and I'll get
you plenty of shots at big blues. But that fish
today—"

"Don't even say it." Hawker laughed. "It'll
make us both miserable."

As Watson worked the pleasure craft
through the reef to the dock, Sha came above.
She was no longer a nun. She had metamor-
phosed, trading her habit for satin shorts and

open-neck blouse, looking lean and lithe and beautiful with her black hair hanging down.

Watson looked at her and was speechless. He almost failed to back onto the dock quickly enough, and the boat hit the pilings hard.

Sha already had both of their bags, and as she stepped off nimbly, she waved gaily at Watson.

"Christ," Watson whispered to Hawker. "That is the most beautiful nun I've ever seen. What is she, in disguise or something? What a bloody great body—"

"Don't say anything you might regret, Captain," Hawker warned, trying not to smile.

"I just don't see how you're going to spend them long hot nights on a tropical island without . . . without . . ." Watson almost blushed. "Without, you know. . . ."

Hawker stepped off the boat onto the wharf. "Discipline," he said, pushing the bow of the boat away again. "I'll just think clean thoughts and remind myself what a bad habit that would be to get into."

"Good luck with that!" Watson called after Hawker.

At dusk they flew low over the Pacific, the atoll reefs colorful mounds of green and blue.

The pilot gave Kira-Kira a wide berth, then banked north until a tiny island of white beach and jungle, all encircled by coral, came into view. They came in at palm-tree level and landed on the beach.

Hawker jumped out, took the bags and Sha's hand, and ran away from the chopper.

The pilot waited while Hawker trotted quickly into the interior, found the fallen tree that had been described to him, looked beneath it and pulled the tarps away.

Hidden there were four big crates. Using his Randall attack knife to knock the lid off one of them, Hawker saw that the weaponry he had wanted was there. He trotted back to the beach and gave the thumbs-up sign.

The pilot returned the sign, and the helicopter lifted away, banking and then disappearing into the blood-red glow of sunset.

The silence that remained was complete. They could hear nothing but the wash and whoosh of the surf beyond the reef and the chatter of monkeys far back in the jungle.

Sha stood watching the chopper disappear, looking a little forlorn. Hawker said, "It's going to be okay, Sha. There's everything we need here. Food, a gas stove, a tent. Even a radio."

She looked up at him. "Just one tent?"

"I'll sleep out on the beach. Don't worry."

"Good," she said. "That good. I get dinner ready. You light stove."

The vigilante opened the three remaining crates. He took out the tent and lit the stove.

eleven

THREE DAYS ON a tropical island, just the two of them.

Cwong's shipment would be delivered two days late. Hawker got the message on the portable UHF radio the agency had provided. He got the message in simple code during his first check-in time. He called someone—he didn't know who, or where—at 7 A.M. and 7 P.M. every day.

Since Harper had wanted to arrive on Kira-Kira the day before the delivery, that meant they'd have an extra day to fill on this tiny unnamed island.

Hawker insisted they not spend the days doing nothing.

Boredom was a killer—making people slow

and sluggish, obstructing the thinking process. Hawker put them on a schedule and insisted they stick to it.

Every morning, the vigilante ran. He ran on the beach and even hacked a trail through the jungle so he could run there too. He wanted to run in the water, but there were too many sea urchins.

Hawker even got Sha to run. She wore a pale-orange French string bikini that made her look as dark as a Negro. Hawker could see her ribs undulate, could see the taut buttocks muscles flex with each stride, could see her round breasts bounce and fall, the nipples sharpening with the rhythmic caress of the thin bikini top.

He could smell the musky-sweet girl-odor of her when the sweat started pouring; it was a different odor than Occidental women produced, spicier, more delicate. That odor hit Hawker hard, making him want her so much that he had to charge on ahead and leave her behind, for fear of starting something he would later regret.

Every day it was like that.

Sha never asked why. Sha accepted everything without complaint or question. She would talk about the weather or the birds she had seen on her run. Once she talked about a great black shark she had seen working inside the reef line. Big as a horse, she had said.

There were sharks, all right.

Plenty of sharks.

Every day, during the glassy afternoon calm, the vigilante swam half a mile out to the reef with mask and fins. He would dive the reef, enjoying the sumptuous Disney World colors of both the coral and the exotic fish.

Hawker had made a Hawaiian sling, which he used the first day to spear a few fish for dinner. But the sharks immediately had come in on him, come in fast over the reef, their heads swinging and ready to hit.

Hawker had dropped the fish, letting the sharks take them. He had swum slowly away from the bloody frenzy.

He never speared fish after that. He used the sling to gig lobster, but nothing else.

The sharks didn't bother him anymore. It got so that he enjoyed watching them, even the big oceanic white tips, come gliding in over the reef like aircraft.

Sha spent the first and second afternoons finishing a palm-thatched hut, a place for him to sleep off the ground. He protested, telling her they would only be staying a couple of days, that he didn't need anything that nice.

"You nice to give me tent," she insisted. "I be nice back."

She made the roof out of palm thatch, weaving it together tightly. It kept out most of the rain during the afternoon showers. To make him a bed, as well as a place for him to sit, she lashed limbs together. Hawker had to admit it was a nice place to read when the rain came pounding down in a silver sheet, very cool and dry. Plus, it smelled great.

In the two hours of light after supper, Hawker insisted they go over the charts. They reviewed them again and again, picking out primary and secondary rendezvous points in case they got separated and each had to make it off Kira-Kira alone.

Privately the vigilante had been trying to come up with a plan to hit Cwong not only on Kira-Kira but at his two drop islands, Tongo and Mokii, too.

Trouble was, those islands were nearly thirty nautical miles away over open sea—not far in a car, but a hell of a long way to go at night in unfamiliar waters.

The inflatable boat and engine in one of the crates was no toy: an Avon Military MKII, seventeen feet long with an aluminum deck, an inflatable keel, and a seventy-horsepower Yamaha outboard. The literature said the boat weighed only four hundred pounds, and Hawker guessed it would do maybe fifty miles an hour in a pinch.

He decided to leave out the aluminum decking, in order to cut the weight of the boat to under two hundred pounds, not counting the engine. That would add a little speed and make it easier to drag up and hide on the beach.

But they had supplied him with only thirty gallons of gas in five six-gallon tanks. If he and Sha had to make a long emergency run from Kira-Kira, they'd need every drop of the fuel. They couldn't afford to risk it in a sixty-mile round-trip sabotage run.

Finally, though, Hawker hit upon an idea. It meant waiting maybe an extra day on Kira-Kira before he attacked, but that would give them that much more time to familiarize themselves with Cwong's compound. He didn't tell Sha anything about the plan. But he did get her to help with the assembly of the Avon, making sure she knew how to run it, switch fuel tanks, get the thing started with the pull rope, and use the choke.

He didn't want her stranded on that island if something happened to him.

They left for Kira-Kira just before sunset on the third day, heading out into big turquoise rollers with Hawker at the throttle and Sha hunched on the bow, wearing a baggy black wool sweater. All the weaponry he could possibly need was packed neatly beneath a tarp, everything tied down to the raft. He had made his last check-in call on the portable UHF and packed that too—although he wasn't sure why. If he got into trouble on Kira-Kira, there was no way anyone would—or could—bail him out.

Hawker found the most comfortable speed, finding the rhythm of the sea beneath. He opened the rubber boat up once, just to see what it would do. The boat seemed to gather buoyancy as it gained velocity, launching itself off the top of every wave. It jarred their kidneys and loosened their teeth, screaming along at what was easily fifty miles an hour.

The speed was there, all right, if they ever needed it.

Hawker dropped back to a comfortable thirty or so, checking his big luminescent diver's wrist compass every now and again, enjoying the bronze-streaked sky and the fresh sea wind in his face. It was a big ocean out there. It made him feel tiny, and he enjoyed that too.

Kira-Kira lifted out of the horizon almost immediately. It was a lot closer than the vigilante had expected. He slowed the craft enough so they would approach under darkness. They actually had to stop and drift for a while, waiting, not wanting to take the least chance of being seen. Then they peeled way out around to the back side, the side of the island with a rind of beach and then jungle climbing up the sheer mountain wall.

Sha pointed and said, "That the place. That the place where I come out when a little girl. Find my way out to that beach, saw some fishermens in a boat. They pick me up when see me wave at them, take me to next island. Take me five days to get to New Guinea. Little girl begging rides on boats."

When it was dark, Hawker took the boat in over the reef. The reef came up within two feet of the surface on low tide, and the surf was huge. They had a wild surfboard ride in, with Hawker gritting his teeth, scared he'd lose it, pitchpole, and dump all his gear.

But they made it.

It was completely dark now, stars glittering above, a three-quarter moon making the beach milky white.

While Hawker pulled the boat up and cut branches and banana leaves to camouflage it in the jungle, Sha strung the jungle hammocks.

They ate a cold supper of C-rations, burying the cans. Afterward they sat shoulder to shoulder in the chilly wind, watching the surf roll in. Hawker put his arm around her once and held her for a time. She seemed comfortable enough, leaning her head against him. But then she broke away suddenly.

"I go my hammock now. Very sleepy. I take you across mountain tomorrow. Okay?"

"That's fine," said Hawker. "Just fine. But do

me a favor. Take the revolver I gave you to bed. I may go out in the boat for a while."

"You not do anything crazy? You not try spy on Cwong this soon?"

"I won't do anything crazy," Hawker said. "I'm just restless, that's all. I'd go for a walk, but this place is probably thick with snakes."

Sha said, "Snakes last thing you got to worry about on this island."

Hawker pulled on his black wool sweater and darkened his face with military grease-paint. He loaded mask, fins, scuba gear, and the explosives he would need into the boat. He placed the Colt Commando assault rifle, fully loaded, at his side. Then he pushed the boat back out into the water, hopped in, and started the engine.

He didn't relish the idea of fighting his way through the surf to the other side of the reef, so he decided to try running inside the atoll. The worst thing that could happen was that he'd knock the propeller off on a coral head—and he carried an extra propeller. Besides, the roar of the surf would help cover the noise of his engine.

Hawker ran through the darkness, gauging his position by the white surf line and the dark coast. He ran until he saw the lights of what he knew from the aerial photographs marked

Cwong's big wharf. The vigilante ran still another half mile until the lights began to
sharpen, then found an opening in the jungle.
He swung the inflatable in, pulled it up, hid it,
strapped the scuba tank to his back, carried
mask fins and explosives back into the shallow
water, and began walking toward the lights.

He had stopped farther away than he had to.
Indeed, Hawker found himself walking for
nearly half an hour before coming to the fenc-
ing and the bright vapor lights that separated
Cwong's compound from the jungle. He could
see the big wharf clearly, with its huge loading
crane and two forty-foot plus diesel cargo craft
moored there.

If Cwong's men were going to make a big
drug delivery tomorrow night, they would certainly use those two boats.

Hawker's whole plan to damage Tongo and
Mokii at the same time he was hitting Cwong
hinged on that assumption.

He hoped to hell he was right.

He checked the time on his Seiko Sub-
mariner: 9:27 P.M. Then he took out two magnetic thermite clock-activated bombs and
carefully set the detonators for 9:30 P.M. the
next day.

According to his intelligence, the boats were
to make their deliveries at 9 P.M. Half an hour
would allow for late starts.

Carrying a diving light and the explosives in a canvas pack, Hawker waded backward into the water. The only other weapon he carried was his large stainless-steel Randall attack knife, the one made for him by Bo Randall in Orlando, Florida. He had that strapped to his calf.

The water covered him, green sparks erupting around his hands every time he moved them. These were bioluminescent microscopic creatures, tracing his path.

That wasn't good. Hawker decided he would have to swim the half mile to the reef, letting the rough water cover his trail.

When he got to the shallow inside edge of the reef, he poked his head up. He had roughly another quarter mile to go to get to the boats. Hawker took a bearing with the wrist compass, then dove back into the water.

It seemed to take forever to get there, traveling through the blackness. He kept expecting a shark to nail him at any moment. Finally, though, there were huge weird shapes ahead of him: the cement pilings of the wharf.

Hawker was in deeper water now, traveling along the bottom, his eyes locked on the green glow of the compass. When he saw the pilings, he relaxed a little.

When he began to ascend slowly, he spotted

the bowl shapes of the boat hulls above him in the glimmer of moonlight.

He slid the canvas bag, the one with the explosives, off his shoulder.

twelve

HAWKER REACHED UP and touched the bottom of one of the boats with his hand, feeling the thin coating of slime and the occasional barnacle.

They had both been hauled recently, scraped and painted. Not a good sign. It might mean that Cwong took good care of his equipment, that he was a stickler for details. Perhaps he ran a tight camp. Hawker didn't like having neatness freaks as adversaries. They were dangerous people, because they usually prepared for everything. It was damn hard to catch them out.

Hawker followed the hull of the second boat until he came to the twin drive shafts that angled out through the stuffing box, ending in two giant brass props. There he rested for a moment, breathing easily through the single hose regulator. He could hear the chain-rattle clink of the boats above, washing against the quay. He could hear the woodwind grunts of fish, the pop and crackle of pistol shrimp. The silent undersea world wasn't really so silent after all.

After the vigilante had rested, he pulled open the plastic zipper on the canvas bag. Careful that his air tank didn't clank against the steel hull of the boat as he worked, Hawker removed one of the four magnetic bombs. He used the tiny underwater light on his wrist to check the timer once more. The twenty-four-hour dials were set for 2130 hours, 9:30 P.M. the next day.

If things worked as he hoped, the boats would each go to their respective docks on Tongo and Mokii. Then, while they were being unloaded, the bombs would disable each vessel, maybe taking some of Cwong's elite guards up with them. Cutting off their return to Kira-Kira would give Hawker more time to concentrate on destroying the complex there.

Hawker placed the first bomb just astern of midship, under where the engine and fuel tank would probably be. Swimming to the second vessel, he clamped the round platter magnet in approximately the same area.

The bombs were filled with three thousand grams of thermite, a composition that would explode, then burn, for about four minutes at more than 3,600 degrees. At that temperature, even underwater, it would burn through two solid inches of armor plating.

If the explosion didn't set the boats on fire, the thermite hitting the fuel tanks certainly would.

Hawker swam into the eerie dark maze of cement pilings beneath the wharf. He swam slowly, taking his time, careful not to brush against the barnacles. When he felt something heavy hit against him, a great weight sliding by, Hawker whirled around.

He forced himself not to panic in the darkness. Sticking his left hand out to fend off any attacker, he drew his big Randall knife in his right.

And nothing happened.

Not a sound.

Hawker took a chance: He twisted the lens of the dive light and shone it around quickly.

He didn't see a thing.

But something had come past him, all right. There was no doubt about that. Something big; something that knew he was there.

It could only be one thing. One of the big open-ocean sharks had to be cruising the shallows. It had probably sensed his vibrations and brushed past to see if he was edible. Hawker hoped to hell the fish had not liked what it felt.

He switched off the light, pressed his back against one of the pilings, and waited awhile longer. He expected to be hit at any moment, to feel the deadly crush of an angry shark's jaws.

Hawker waited and waited, until he realized it was useless to wait anymore. If the shark wanted him, the shark would get him. There was absolutely nothing he could do about it.

Hawker pushed away from the piling, worked his way carefully to the area he guessed would put him beneath the big cargo derrick, then surfaced.

He had come up short. He was still beneath the front side of the quay. Above him he could hear voices—indistinct voices. They were probably speaking in Vietnamese; he didn't understand a word of that.

Hawker decided to stay on the surface. The big Rocket fins pushed him to the great cement base of the derrick. There he placed both of the remaining thermite bombs, setting the timers for 10 P.M. the following night. 2200 hours.

If luck was with them, he and Sha could get across the volcanic mountain and into Cwong's camp by then. Hit them from both sides, that was Hawker's plan. And the explosions would make them think the attack was coming from the direction of the sea.

The voices above him were louder now, more emotional.

He wondered what was going on.

No way was he going to stick around and try to find out. He pulled his mask down, submerged . . . and that's when something hit him from the side, something big.

He thought it was a shark. . . .

All the little sensory nodes searched frantically, his brain checking every limb, expecting to find his legs gone, his chest ripped open.

But there wasn't much pain. Just that sense of being held, of being wrestled downward toward the bottom.

As the vigilante tried to pull his arms free, he was aware of a tube of light swinging crazily back and forth, swinging from the dark object that held him.

It was then that he finally realized he was being held by a man, another diver who had a flashlight attached to his wrist. It only took a microsecond for Hawker to realize that the diver had probably been on an underwater patrol and had spotted Hawker's light. Undoubtedly he had taken advantage of the overhead dock lights to hit Hawker from below, zeroing in on the silhouette the vigilante must have thrown.

Damn! Cwong's men were good.

The first thing the diver had done was rip the regulator away from Hawker's mouth; the vigilante suddenly realized that, in his fear, he had been holding his breath, not even noticing that he no longer had a source of oxygen. Fear can do that to a man.

But now Hawker had to do something. And the truth was that he was actually relieved he had been attacked by a man, not the shark that had nudged him earlier.

Now all he had to do was break the man's grip before he drowned.

The diver had both of Hawker's arms pinned against his sides, driving him sideways, deeper and deeper. Hawker had been struggling, but now he forced himself to go limp, staging a total lack of resistance. The assailant reacted just as Hawker hoped he would, loosening his grip to readjust his position. The vigilante used that small opening to rip his right arm free, find the diver's face, and yank the man's face mask and regulator away.

Now Hawker was loose, swimming wildly toward the surface and finally finding his own regulator. Hawker jammed it into his mouth and found just enough residual air in his lungs to blow the exhaust ports clear.

The vigilante was taking a few small draughts of the bottled air, looking at the glimmer of lights above, when he was caught from behind again.

Except for the wild swinging beam of the flashlight, it was like fighting a barely visible dark blob. Hawker got his arm locked around what he knew must be the diver's head. He tried feverishly to find the Randall knife in the calf scabbard, but missed when the diver got his hand around Hawker's throat . . . and then he felt a stinging pain along his cheek.

The diver had a knife of his own. He had it out and was trying to use it.

Hawker used both feet to fend the man off, kicking away. He saw the beam of light come up and hold on him, temporarily blinding him. The diver could see him, but all the vigilante could see was the powerful light coming closer and closer. The man couldn't miss again with his knife. After all, he now had the advantage of being able to see.

But then, in the narrow bloom of light, the vigilante saw something else appear, something he never thought he would be relieved to see: a huge black shape coming out of the gloom. Hawker saw the wide missile-shaped head, tiny eyes, and jagged wide grin of a shark.

The shark came sailing into the light, head

wagging back and forth. It disappeared for a moment, but then all Hawker saw was the gray belly-blur as the great fish rolled toward the diver who had attacked him.

The beam of light strapped to the diver's wrist made wild, crazy circles, spinning as he spun. It stabilized for a moment, showing both of the diver's hands clawing furiously at the shark's head. It was an unsettling sight, especially since by this time the shark had taken the diver's whole chest into its mouth. Hawker shuddered as the shark swam away with the man, the horrible picture getting smaller and smaller as the fish sped away. Dark smoke, like dust, boiled out of the fish's mouth. The vigilante knew it was blood.

Hawker swam instinctively to one of the big pilings, clinging to it for cover. The crazy fear that there might be two sharks around, not just one, entered his mind.

Finally, when his brain began to work again, he knew he had to get away. The men on the wharf might have seen the lights, heard the commotion. They might be expecting their patrol diver to surface at any moment.

He had to get away from the pier, shark or no shark.

Hawker took a big breath through the regulator, steeling himself. Then he swam back toward the dark water, back toward the reef where the big fish congregated. He swam until his watch told him he'd gone far enough, then headed into shallow water.

When he was finally back in knee-deep water, wading toward the inflatable boat he had hidden in the jungle, a nausea came over him that he could not possibly ignore. Turning his head away, he vomited salt water and bile and something else, something ripe and musky from deep down inside his gut.

It was the taste of fear.

Hawker knew the taste; he had tasted it before. But somehow he couldn't remember it ever having been as horrible as this.

thirteen

SHA CAME ONTO the beach as he pulled the inflatable toward the jungle. She was digging her fist at her eyes and yawning, her lean, long-haired figure looking dazzling in the moonlight. The only clothes she wore were a T-shirt and shorts.

Still, Hawker hardly paid any attention. He hadn't felt so tired since the first three days of Coronado.

"Where you been?" she asked. "I been worried about you. Why take so long?"

"Went out for a boat ride. Just restless. Go on back to sleep, Sha."

"You not do nothing dumb, no? You not try go around island. Many guns there. Many men. Boom-boom, shoot you, no kidding."

"I didn't go around the island, Sha. There's nothing to worry about. You look sleepy. Go on back and get some rest."

"They got machine up there. Things go around and around, tell them when big boats get too close. See pictures on screen. Very dangerous you go out alone like that. I worry, could hardly sleep."

Hawker had the Randall out and was cutting more tree limbs in the moonlight, hiding the boat. He stopped long enough to look up at the woman. "Are you sure you haven't already been to America? You sound more and more like half the women I knew back in Chicago."

Sha put her hands on her lean hips. "What that mean? I should feel bad 'cause you go out, make it so I can no sleep—" She stopped in midsentence, her mouth open. "What happen to your face? You bleeding!" Immediately Sha was at Hawker's side, one hand on his shoulder, the other inspecting the slash on his cheek.

"Ouch." Hawker pulled away. "Damn it, Sha, that hurts. Get your fingers off it."

She backed away. "You did go around island, didn't you? Had big fight, I bet. Now Cwong know we here. He be looking for us. I think—"

Hawker snapped at her: "Do me a favor— don't think, okay, Sha? I'll do the thinking. You're getting paid to do just one thing. Remember, that was your rule, not mine."

Sha stuck her lower lip out, pouting. "Need bandage on face. Cut bad. Very bad. I promise ask no more questions, but let me fix face. You ugly 'nough, don't need no more scars to make you more uglier."

Hawker stopped working for a moment, looked at her again, and almost laughed. "Okay," he said finally. "You fix my cut. If that makes you happy, go ahead and get the first-aid kit. I'll finish up here."

The woman came trotting back with bandages and a Coleman lantern. After sitting the vigilante down on the Avon, she lit the lantern. The Coleman made its steady hiss, throwing a warm circle of light into the jungle around them.

Moths and insects found the light almost immediately, battering themselves against it. Hawker watched the insects, wondering why they were unfailingly attracted to the very thing that was the source of their destruction. The insects made him wonder about the woman. She could have played it safe. Could have stayed away. Yet she had returned to the island where her father had been killed. Where she had almost been destroyed as a little girl. And she did it on her own. She had even refused money, still not knowing he had made the deposit in her account.

She worked on his face with obvious skill—

cleaning it, putting on sulfur powder, cutting butterfly bandages to fit. She drew the skin together and pressed gauze and tape into place.

"You've done this before," Hawker said. "I'm not surprised. Working at The Saigon, you probably got a lot of practice in first aid, huh? Probably a fight every time an American walked in there."

The woman smiled at him ruefully. "You very funny, you know? Always say funny things. Tell me one thing. Why you think I dumb?"

"Dumb? I don't think you're dumb."

"You tell me not think no more. Very angry. Treat me like I too dumb to think. Make me know my place. I like you in restaurant 'cause you let me think. Say you trust my judgment. Now, all sudden you just like all men at restaurant. Very bossy. Make me feel too dumb to help."

"Oh, boy," said Hawker, but feeling guilty anyway. "All I meant was—"

She was standing, packing the first-aid stuff away. "What you mean was, Sha no talk. No think. Stay in my place. You say I only get paid to do one thing. That what you really want?"

"Not at all," Hawker said. As he said it, he wondered why nature seemed to give women an inborn ability to reduce men—any man—to apologetic boobs within a matter of seconds, regardless of who was right or who was wrong. "I want you to think," he said.

"I think you're very bright and appreciate any advice you can give me. I shouldn't have said what I did. I'm sorry. And I'm sorry I snapped at you."

"You really mean it? You really think me smart?"

"Sure do. Yep. You're a very bright lady."

"You really like me give advice? You want me to be like partner? Equal partner?"

"Partner?" said Hawker. "Sure. Sure, and I want you to give advice too. Honest."

"Then here my advice," Sha said.

"I thought we'd get to this." He smiled.

"My advice is stay away from other side of island till I show you only good way get there! Don't be such big dummy! I no like big dummy for partner!" Sha whirled away, stomping off toward the jungle hammocks.

Hawker released a heavy sigh. Twisting the gas knob on the Coleman, he watched the light fade. "Christ," he said wearily.

They left for Cwong's military complex in the morning.

Hawker awoke later than normal. The sun was just over the palm trees that arched in a line away from the beach. He could hear the sounds of birds squawking and monkeys chattering through the jungle.

Hawker spread open the hammock and crawled from beneath the netting. He scratched his head and immediately winced. His jaw hurt like hell. His shoulders ached. Even his joints ached. His hands had been cut on barnacles, something he didn't even notice last night.

He smiled wryly. Getting older sure was a bitch. Five years ago he would have come through the whole ordeal without noticing the abrasions and bruises. Now he felt as if he'd been beaten with a bat.

Hawker stretched painfully, yawned, and looked around.

Sha's hammock was empty.

He walked out into the little clearing near the beach, making sure no boats were out there to see him. Sha's tracks led down the beach. He followed them.

Her tracks cut in abruptly toward a sheer wall of volcanic rock. Hawker could hear the distant splash of water and someone singing. It was Sha's voice.

He worked his way through the palm trees until he came to a clearing. A small river came down the side of the mountain and fell off a ledge. A waterfall. There Sha stood, naked in the pool of water below, washing her hair.

There was a bar of soap on the rock beside her and a coconut with its top whacked off.

Hawker stood watching, enjoying the sight of her, the tautness of her body, the leanness of her hips, the small firm breasts with their brown nipples, the glistening pubic thatch, long and black. He watched as she threw her hair over her shoulder, like a dark sodden rope, then picked up the coconut and worked the coconut water into her hair.

He felt like a snoop. Hawker didn't like the feeling, but he didn't want to leave either. It was a nice thing to see, her standing beneath the waterfall, a true island beauty.

Pushing his way out into the clearing, Hawker stopped beside the pool, ten yards from her. "How you doing, partner?" he said.

"What? Hey!"

Hawker laughed at the way she tried to cover herself—pulling her right knee up, throwing an arm across her breasts, trying to cover her pubis with an open hand.

"Let me know when you're done with the shower, partner. I'm next." The vigilante turned and walked back toward their camp. "And don't use all the hot water!" he called over his shoulder.

Sha came back into camp a few minutes later looking sheepish.

"All done?" Hawker asked, smiling.

"You spy on me. Watch me naked."

"That's right, I spied on you. You were too pretty not to watch."

That seemed to please her, but she tried not to show it. Indeed, she slapped at him as she walked by. "I get stuff ready to go while you shower."

"You no come and watch?" Hawker grinned, mimicking her.

"No! I got manners. I no watch!" She paused and grinned back. "Beside, I already see you."

"And you didn't like what you saw?"

She just walked away, flapping her hand at him.

It took them half an hour to pack the gear they might need into backpacks with frames.

Hawker carried the Colt Commando slung over his shoulder.

He noticed that the woman had stuck the little snub-nosed revolver into the big pocket of her shorts.

For half an hour they walked, avoiding the mountain. As they made their way through the jungle, hacking at vines, monkeys and birds scolded them from the high trees.

Hawker kept an eye on Sha as they went, watching her expression. She seemed confused at first. That worried him. It had been a long time since she had found her "secret" path across the mountain. She had been a little girl then, probably frightened half out of her mind.

He had to force himself not to second-guess her, ignoring the persistent urge to keep asking if she recognized anything. Hawker knew that pressure froze the memory banks, and he wanted her memory to be at its best.

Gradually the confusion left her face. She began to move faster through the dense foliage. Once she stopped and looked at a huge black tree, one of the biggest trees Hawker had ever seen. Its trunk was the size of a two-car garage, maybe two hundred feet high. She peered up and said, "Yes. This I remember. This great tree. When a little girl, I rest here, wanting so bad someone come and help me."

Sha touched the tree fondly, then moved on without another word.

The "secret" passage was a great crevasse in the mountain. It began as a cave opening hardly wide enough for Hawker to get his shoulders through. Sha simply walked toward a sheer rock ledge covered with vines and leaves, began poking at the vines, pushing them away, and there it appeared, this crack in the earth. Hawker wondered how in the hell she found it, how she possibly could have remembered. But somewhere in that little girl's memory, the way of her escape from the bad man of Kira-Kira was forever etched.

On hands and knees now, he crawled behind her into the dark cave. He took out his little flashlight, holding it in his teeth.

"Why you need light?" she asked once. "Nothing to see."

The cave broadened, becoming huge. The floor was covered with water, the walks slick with slime.

Hawker switched off the flashlight and saw that light filtered in from someplace, he couldn't tell where. The ceiling of the cave was so high, there were probably cracks all along the top of it.

It was rough walking. Volcanic litter covered the floor. Suddenly Hawker saw something on one of the walls and shined his light. Huge ceremonial faces stared down at him, Polynesian-type Kon Tiki faces. Perhaps they had been drawn by some tribesman a hundred or even a thousand years ago. The faces of the Polynesian gods had eerie eyes, fierce and accusing.

After more than an hour of walking, they came out into daylight, although they still remained in the crevasse. Grass and roots formed a roof over much of the crevasse, probably making it impossible to see in from above. Twice they passed human skeletons, shattered skulls testifying to the fact.

Sha hurried by the skeletons, hands against

her chest, as if they might reach up and bite her.

Finally the crevasse funneled into another, narrower cave opening. It was strictly a hands-and-knees journey at this point, the backpacks barely fitting through. Hawker said, "How in the world did you get up the courage to come through this thing when you were just a kid? I keep expecting to put my hand on a snake or a rat or something."

From the darkness came Sha's voice. "You never meet Cwong. Nothing so scary as Cwong. After being with him, nothing frighten me."

But the narrow tunnel did not last for long. Ahead, Hawker could see a pinpoint of daylight—tiny at first, then getting broader, whiter. Sha pushed away dirt and roots and grass, and Hawker stepped out behind her into the smokey daylight of jungle.

Behind them was the sheer volcanic wall of the mountain.

Before them were the steel buildings and wooden shacks and chain-link fence of the complex.

"There it is," Sha said with an involuntary shiver. "That where you go tonight. That where you kill Cwong."

fourteen

THEY RESTED, THE sun a pale bubble over the glittering Pacific. It leached steam from the jungle. Even the monkeys seemed to doze.

Hawker slept beneath a huge tree with elephant-ear leaves. He would awaken occasionally, his eyes searching for sentries. Once he awoke to see Sha looking at him.

"Hi," he said.

"Hi. I thinking."

"Oh? About what?"

"About place I make for you, back on island. Place with thatch roof. Very nice, huh?"

"Yes," said Hawker. "Very nice. I liked it a lot."

She stirred, uncomfortable. "Just think

might be nice go back there . . . you and me."

Hawker raised himself on one elbow. "You and me? You in the tent, me in the little hut?"

She looked away. "No. Just you and me."

Hawker smiled, dropping back down. He slept until someone shook him away from a dream in which he was with another woman in another jungle, not so long ago.

The vigilante sat bolt upright. "What—"

Sha was kneeling over him, shaking him gently. "You tell me wake you when sun goes down. It time now."

Hawker stood up to see one of the most stunning sunsets he'd ever seen: a huge orange ball, streaked with brass and purple, melting into the sea.

He stretched and yawned. "You okay?" Sha asked. "Maybe we should wait. Wait maybe tomorrow?"

Hawker looked at his watch: 8:17 P.M. The thermite bombs he had planted on the boats would be going off in about forty minutes. The bombs he had planted under the derrick would explode in just over an hour.

"No reason to wait," said Hawker. "I've been looking forward to this too long to wait. You know what you're supposed to do?"

"Maybe I should come with you. Maybe you need help."

Hawker shook his head. "No. You are to do absolutely nothing. Understand? You stay right here no matter what you see or what you hear. When I get away, coming up the mountain, I'll blink my flashlight three times. But don't shine any signal in return. Just watch for me. Yell if you have to. I'll probably be moving fast, and there may be somebody after me. If it looks like you're in any danger at all, get the hell back through the passage. Take the boat, the exact headings I gave you. I'll make it on my own just fine. You understand?"

"I understand," she said, "but I no like. Should come with you. Maybe help."

Hawker had already set out the gear he would need. He finished greasing his face, and pulled the black wool watch cap on over his dark hair. "You've already helped. I mean that. And when we get back, after we rest up a little and all this stuff dies down, we'll take a trip back to that little island. Spend a few days in your grass hut."

"You mean that? For sure, you mean that?"

"Sure I mean it," he said.

Hawker shouldered his gear, turned, and walked down through the jungle, toward Cwong's camp.

The vigilante waited outside the high chain-link fence, in the trees beyond the ten-yard killing area on the outside of the complex. He watched the lights of the complex come on all at once as the generator kicked on. Hawker could see the guards change demeanor, relaxing a little with darkness and lighting cigarettes.

Cwong certainly had no shortage of guards. The backside of the chain-link fence stretched maybe a quarter mile along the rear of the compound. Four guards paced that area in pairs.

Hawker assumed there were four guards for each side of the complex, probably more out front by the wharf and still more by the arsenal.

The ground inside the fence was roughly mowed scrub and sand, with a few palm trees. Beyond the fence were six small wooden houses, probably guards' quarters. Beyond those were two large storehouse areas. Hawker knew from his intelligence briefing that off to the left of that was the camouflaged storage area for Cwong's arsenal.

From the vigilante's position, the area looked like a plain of low jungle. Cwong had probably covered the area with netting and vegetation. Beneath the netting would probably be enough stolen ordnance to equip a small army.

Hawker knew that he would have to keep

reminding himself that Cwong's men would certainly not lack firepower. He would have to hit them by surprise. Hit them hard and fast. Somehow he had to find Cwong, eliminate him, and get the hell out. It would be plenty tough: This organization was like some great writhing creature with Cwong for a brain.

Eliminate the brain, kill it, and the creature would die.

Lying in the jungle, watching the compound, Hawker thought once again about Cwong the man—what he would look like, what his expression might be when he looked up to see an executioner staring him in the face. He also thought once again about Sha as a little girl, how it must have been for her to be taken by such a disgusting creature. Hawker felt his grip tighten on the Colt Commando he held in his hands.

He checked his watch again: 8:45. The thermite bombs would soon turn the two cargo ships into fireballs. He wondered how the people on the islands of Tongo and Mokii would react. They'd probably be pleased—glad that their keeper had been hurt in some way.

As the second pair of guards strolled by and disappeared into the orange haze of the distant vapor lights, the vigilante took a deep breath, got to his feet, and sprinted to the fence. Quickly he took out the voltage tester he carried in the pocket of his green wool limey commando pants. He touched one prong to the fence and the other to the metal post.

The light did not come on.

Surprisingly, the fence was not electrified.

But it would certainly be wired to some kind of burglar alarm system . . . or would it?

The fence was six feet high with concertina wire on top. Hawker reached up, running his hands along the top bar. He felt a flat coated wire. Looking both ways to make sure the guards were still far enough away, he took out a long wire with alligator clips on both ends. Ever so gently, Hawker pressed both clips into the wire, then snipped it. He listened intently for bells and alarms and sirens to go off, but there were none.

Hawker hurried back into the jungle once more as the guards approached, passed, and faded away. There was still no indication that he'd set off an alarm. So far, so good. He could feel the adrenaline-flutter deep in the abdomen that he always felt before starting a tough mission. It was a good feeling.

Hawker took out the big wire cutters and sprinted back to the fence. He cut the heavy chain link between the alligator clips, skittered under the wire, then dove behind a clump of coconut palms as the guards returned and passed.

In his backpack he carried eight pounds of military-issue plastic explosives. He had already molded the yellow catalyst into the blue claylike explosives, kneading it until it turned green. All the explosives needed now were the radio-activated blasting detonators.

The vigilante slid out of the pack, took three half-pound chunks out, broke each in two, then sprinted to the first of the six wooden houses that housed Cwong's elite guard.

He poked his head up to the window of one. Inside, a half-dozen men sat cross-legged on the floor. There was a pile of money in the middle of the floor, American currency, and the men were hooting and laughing as they rolled dice.

Hawker watched them for a moment, then ducked back down. The houses were built up on cement blocks. He took a chunk of the plastic explosive and stuck it beneath the house, then inserted the detonator.

As he got back to his feet, he heard the faint rustle of footsteps. Turning to look, he fell backward as a wide, dark figure dove into him. The figure was swinging something, something long and bright, reflecting the faint camp lights.

One of the guards had found him and was now trying to kill him with a knife.

fifteen

FALLING BACKWARD, THE vigilante let the guard's momentum carry him over his shoulders. The stranger somersaulted over onto his back.

The guard landed with a *whoof* that knocked the air right out of him, which might have been the luckiest thing that had happened to Hawker for a long time. Surely the guard would have called out for help if he could have found the air to speak.

The vigilante kicked the man once in the side of the neck, but the soft heel of the Nikes he wore only stunned him. The guard responded by rolling to his knees, brandishing the knife. Hawker kicked the knife from the man's hand, then kicked him hard in the throat.

The guard rolled over, gurgling, clawing at his throat. It would have been enough to disable him for some time. But the vigilante hadn't come to disable.

Coldly and without emotion, he drew the Randall knife from the calf holster and drove the big saw-edge blade into the man's right eye and twisted. He pulled the knife out and cleaned the blade in the earth before reholstering it.

The guard lay in the darkness, twitching in his own blood.

Once again Hawker scanned the area to make sure no one had heard. He poked his nose up over the window to see the men still playing dice. Then he went to the other houses, looking in each one. Two were empty. There was a total of fifteen men in the other three. Hawker planted explosives only in those three.

He checked the glowing squares of his Seiko watch: 9:14 P.M. The two cargo boats would be burning fireballs by now. In sixteen minutes, the derrick down at the wharf would go up. The vigilante knew he would have to hurry but also knew he had to be extremely cautious, because getting caught now would ruin everything, putting the whole compound on alert.

Cautiously Hawker worked his way across the area to the two big storage barns. He planted plastic explosives and thermite bombs in them, all keyed to the same radio frequency of his detonator. Coming around the corner of the second barn, he almost walked right into two guards who were standing and smoking, their weapons at their feet.

Hawker backed quickly against the wall. He slung the automatic rifle over his shoulder and drew the .45 automatic from its holster. Finding the sound arrester in his pocket, he screwed it on tight. He hoped the sound of the surf and the distant hum of the generator would be enough to cover the noise. But he also knew that he didn't have much choice. If he tried to take them with a knife, one of them would certainly have enough time to call out. Hawker wished he had the Cobra crossbow he had used so often.

Holding the .45 with the barrel by his ear, pointed at the sky, Hawker stepped back around the corner and shot the guards quickly. Two careful shots, that's all it took, the slow slugs knocking their heads back and breaking their necks. The guards were probably dead before the slugs entered their brains.

Hawker stepped out, checking the area carefully before removing the sound arrester and holstering the weapon. Then he was across the clearing, heading for what still looked like a low jungle plain. As he got closer, though, the jungle began to look like a gigantic tent. Hawker could see the support posts, then the dim outline of crates, hundreds of them stacked on top of each other, plus the canvas-color shapes of what had to be cannon and field rocket launchers.

Once he got into the camouflaged area, the vigilante took it a lot more slowly. He couldn't believe there weren't guards all over the place. But he saw none. Maybe Cwong wasn't the perfectionist he had feared. Maybe Cwong thought that the perimeter of his complex was defense enough.

Relieved, the vigilante began to plant his explosives quickly. It seemed a shame to destroy all this complex weaponry paid for by U.S. taxpayers, but those were his orders. He supposed they didn't want Cwong to have a chance to use any of it, or give it away, if the mission failed.

He used plastic explosives on the crates of ammunition and thermite bombs on the field ordnance. He looked for the ATC tank the CIA agents had mentioned but didn't see it. Hawker didn't like that at all.

He hoped to hell Cwong had sold the tank, or at least had shipped it someplace else. The vigilante didn't savor the idea of having to deal with some armor-plated monstrosity that could chase him through the jungle and into the sea.

Hawker almost emptied his pack of explosives on the arsenal. It was a hell of a big area. He had to dodge guards three times, lying on the ground, watching them saunter past. It seemed a little surprising that they hadn't found the dead guards yet, that there hadn't been some kind of alarm sounded.

ker-WHUMPF!!!

Hawker dropped to his belly on the shaking earth.

An orange gaseous ball of fire had just erupted from the wharf area, throwing debris and smoke and flames high up into the South Pacific darkness. The thermite bomb planted beneath the crane had gone off right on schedule. It must have taken up a fuel tank too, judging by the size of the fireball.

Damn. He'd lost track of the time, concentrating so intently on getting the arsenal rigged and watching for guards. He had wanted to be outside Cwong's big house when the bomb went off, to see if the explosion drew out the man's bodyguards. Hawker needed to make sure Cwong didn't leave with them.

Now he'd have to play it by ear.

Throughout the compound men were shouting and running frantically. There was the tinny rattle of automatic weapons fire. That

was good. The guards were reacting emotion-
ally, shooting at ghosts.

The worst thing he could do now was move
slower than the other men, to make a show of
trying not to be seen. With that in mind,
Hawker stood and jogged toward the main
house. He saw a dozen men running en masse
off to the right, but they paid no attention to
him.

Beyond the guards' shacks was a sand lawn,
covered with carefully tended tropical plants,
a fountain, and weird Buddha statuettes. The
vigilante jogged right up to the main house
without being challenged before a man
stepped out of the back door, calling to him to
Vietnamese.

Hawker didn't hesitate: He swung the Colt
Commando around and dropped the man
where he stood with a quick burst of fire. With
all the noise now, no one would even notice.

Next he ran around the side of the house to
the front, getting there just in time to see four
stocky Vietnamese come flying off the huge
antebellum front porch, AK-47s in hand. They
were being urged toward the burning wharf
by an amazingly corpulent Vietnamese in a red
satin smoking jacket. The man's shaved head
made his great gray face look even bigger.

It was Cwong. It *had* to be Cwong. Hawker
would have known even if he hadn't see old

blurry photos of the Viet Cong general taken in the late sixties during the Vietnam war.

He raised his automatic rifle immediately, bringing the steel sights to bear on Cwong's chest.

No. He wouldn't kill him now. Not like this. First he wanted to stare the man in the face, to let him know who his executioner was and why he was about to kill him.

In an instant the opportunity was gone. Cwong slammed the door behind the men, and there was the sound of locks being turned.

But there would be another opportunity.

Hawker would make sure of it.

sixteen

JAMES HAWKER WAITED patiently until
Cwong's bodyguards were out of sight and a
dozen more men in their sloppy khaki Viet
Cong uniforms went sprinting past to reinforce
the wharf area for an attack that would not
come from that direction.

Then he calmly swung up onto the porch
and looked in the big window. He saw a large
room with glistening wood floors, Oriental car-
pets, and ornate furniture. Above a fireplace
made of igneous rock, he could see the big red
banner and yellow star that was the flag of
North Vietnam.

But he saw no people. He didn't see General
Con Ye Cwong, the man who had specialized
in torturing American soldiers during the war

and who now continued his methods of torture long afterward.

Hawker didn't see anyone at all.

He stepped away, glanced around, then kicked in the window. Hawker dove through the opening and came up on his feet holding his assault rifle in his right hand, a U.S. army shrapnel grenade in the other.

Three shots suddenly splintered the wood above his head. The vigilante dropped to his belly and saw a man standing on the balcony above holding some kind of automatic pistol. Hawker didn't have time to aim. He just turned the Commando toward the man, held it on full automatic fire, and let it roar.

The slugs ripped through the man's groin and abdomen, and, screaming, he spilled over the balcony railing onto the floor.

The vigilante was on his feet immediately. He punched out the nearly spent clip and pressed in a fresh one. Sprinting to the steps, his head searching back and forth, he heard some kind of thin wail—the noise of a child crying. Hawker pulled open a door in the hallway to see a small girl lying in the corner of a dark closet. She was small, no older than twelve, with blond hair, and she had her knees pulled up to her chest. The girl was crying.

She looked up when Hawker opened the door, big tear-bleary bright-blue eyes staring right through him. "Don't hurt me, don't hurt me, please," she begged.

Hawker knelt beside her and felt her cringe when he touched her shoulder. "It's okay, it's going to be okay," he said. "Listen to me, sweetheart. I'm going to take you out of here. But we have to move fast."

The girl studied him for a moment, then lost control and leaned forward, sobbing "Want my daddy. Please, I want my daddy!"

Hawker patted her head. "I'll take you to him. But first you have to listen to me. I want you to be brave for just awhile longer. Can you do that?"

The girl wiped her nose. "I can do it," she said. "I want to come with you."

"You will, sweetheart, you will. But right now I want you to run outside. Jump off the side of the porch. The porch is built up on blocks. Crawl under the porch and wait for me. You'll hear some gunshots, probably a lot of them. If I don't come for you within ten minutes after the gunshots stop, I want you to take this flashlight and run right toward the highest part of the mountain behind us. As you go up the first big hill, start blinking this light. Blink three times, off and on. If you keep running, there will be someone there to help you. Can you do that?"

The girl was getting to her feet. "I can do that."

Hawker turned from the closet. He could hear the sound of footsteps on the floor above them, men running. He said, "What's your name?"

"Sarah. Sarah Billings."

"Are there any other children around here, Sarah? Any other children who need help?"

The girl almost lost control again, but steadied herself. "No. Just me."

Hawker took her by the arm and led her quickly down the hall, the Colt Commando vectoring back and forth. He put his little flashlight in her hand and gave her a gentle push. "Then get going, Sarah. And do exactly what I told you to do."

He covered the girl as she climbed nimbly out the window, waiting until he saw her disappear beneath the porch before turning back. And just in time—for now two men on the balcony came sliding into position, AK-47 automatic weapons in their hands. The vigilante opened fire on them before they were able to spot him. One of them was killed instantly, but Hawker watched the other go crawling off holding his belly. The man was screaming in agony.

He waited for just a moment, then charged up the stairs. Heavy footsteps coming down the hall to the right were accompanied by the wild chatter of Vietnamese.

Hawker heard briefly the heavy, deep voice of Cwong, then the slamming of a door. The vigilante poked his head around, then immediately dropped back as several men opened fire on him.

He pulled the pin on the shrapnel grenade and threw it down the hall without looking.

There was a scream, an exclamation, then an explosion that shook the whole foundation of the house.

Hawker looked down the hall again, seeing the torn and writhing bodies through the smokey haze of dust and plaster. He had to shoot two men who reached for their weapons when they saw the tall, lean American at the head of the hall. They dropped to the floor simultaneously, dead.

Then Hawker stood for a moment and listened. He heard only the voice of Cwong coming through the door at the end of the hall; the deep voice was calling out harshly yet was obviously filled with terror. He's probably calling to the guards, Hawker reasoned, wanting to know if the invader has been killed. A slight smile formed on Hawker's lips: The big man was nervous.

Hawker walked quietly toward the door, stopped, and tested the knob.

Automatic weapons fire splintered the door from within. And once again Cwong screamed out, demanding something in Vietnamese, most likely an explanation.

The vigilante slid out of his backpack, searching through it until he found the smoke grenade canister. He pulled the pin on the grenade but held the firing lever in place. Drawing the .45 Smith & Wesson, he emptied the clip at the area beneath the old brass doorknob. Hawker stood back as slugs poured through the wooden door in answer.

Then, in one smooth motion, he kicked the door open and tossed in the smoke grenade. He expected more heavy fire, but there was none. Just a hoarse scream as the grenade went off with a *whoosh*.

Red smoke poured out of the room, and Hawker stepped in cautiously, expecting anything but what he saw.

Cwong sat huddled in the far corner of the room. Hawker could see him dimly through the acrid haze. The Vietnamese villain was sitting holding an empty AK-47 in his lap, blubbering like a huge bald baby. His eyes grew wide as he saw Hawker, and the vigilante continued to walk steadily toward the man despite the outstretched, pleading palms.

"American?" Cwong called out. "You American? Yes, I have many friends who are American! American GIs! Many friends!"

Hawker was standing over him now, the knuckles of his big right hand white on the Colt Commando, his face like a cold mask. Cwong was trying to get to his feet, a big ludicrous grin of terror on his face. "I very rich too," he said. "Much, much money!" He motioned wildly. "Have it right here! Right here in house. I give you all the money you want, GI. Give you much money. Just go 'way! Leave me alone!"

The vigilante's lips barely moved. "I already have all the money I want, sport." Slowly, ever so slowly, he was raising the barrel of the weapon toward Cwong.

Hysterical, Cwong said, "Then drugs! Give you all drugs you want. Drugs, women, get anything for you!"

Hawker said, "I didn't come to take, General Con Ye Cwong. I came to give. Brought you a present from two ladies. Their names are Sha and Sarah, and they both want you to have this. . . ." Hawker shot a short burst and watched the man's face contort in agony, then horror as blood began to pour from his groin. Cwong flipped over on his belly, kicking wildly. "And this is for all your American GI friends," Hawker added, giving the man another short burst in the buttocks. While the fat man screamed and clawed at the floor in pain, Hawker said, "And this is for me," and shot him twice in the spinal cord.

He wanted Cwong's death to be lingering.

seventeen

DOWNSTAIRS NOW, James Hawker could hear the tentative shouts of Cwong's guard. A few of them had obviously caught on that they were not being attacked from the sea.

He turned immediately to the window and looked outside at a coconut palm that threw a feathery silhouette only a few yards away. He opened the window, took the coil of rope from his now nearly empty backpack, and tossed the grappling hook up into the sagging fronds. Hawker had to throw it twice before he got a solid hold.

Then he coiled the remaining rope on the floor, pushed a fresh clip into the Commando, another into the .45 Smith & Wesson, and carried his final two thermite grenades to the head of the stairs.

He looked down to see three men looking back at him. He fired a short burst to protect himself, then tossed down the two grenades.

The heat from the explosions was withering even on the second floor. Hawker retraced his steps to the room and paused for a moment over Cwong. The man was still moaning in pain but was no longer moving. And who could blame him? It's not easy to move with a splintered spinal cord.

Not out of kindness, but out of fear that the man would somehow survive to rebuild his insidious organization, Hawker shot him a final time, this time in the head. Then, without looking back, he slid out the window and climbed down the rope to the ground.

Sarah Billings lay like a frightened animal beneath the porch. She jumped when the vigilante touched her shoulder, nodded when he pressed his finger to his lips, then followed along without making a sound.

Holding the Commando in his right hand and the girl's small palm in his left, he pulled her along toward the back of the complex. Twice they had to stop and hide as soldiers sprinted past.

Then they were outside the huge camouflaged arsenal area, and the chain-link fence was just ahead. Not far to go now.

The vigilante already had his wire cutters in hand as they skidded to a stop at the barrier. Dropping immediately to his knees, he began to cut the heavy wire. He had just made an opening big enough for them to get through when the girl said suddenly, "Hey, what's that? Something's coming!"

Hawker turned to see a massive vehicle near the arsenal grinding toward them, showing one huge spotlight. The spotlight was vectoring back and forth, sweeping nearer to them with every second.

It was the military ATC, the stolen tank come looking for them.

He took the girl's arm, pulled the fence apart, and pushed her through. "Run!" he whispered hoarsely. "Run toward the mountain!"

Then the spotlight was on him, dazzlingly bright. It swept past but immediately returned to hold on him. It blinded him to even look at it.

He was halfway under the fence now, still calling to the disappearing figure of the girl to run, not to stop, while at the same time trying to pull the radio detonator from his pocket. Heavy weapons fire clattered behind him— something really big, probably fifty caliber.

The ATC had him in range and was firing at him.

Finally Hawker pulled himself under the fence. But no sooner had he gotten to one knee with the detonator in his hand, when he felt a tremendous impact hit him high in the left shoulder. The pain stunned him for a moment, and he realized he had been hit. The slugs had knocked him several yards. Amazingly, the detonator lay nearby.

He crawled toward the detonator, feeling something hot on his back, wondering how he could feel anything at all when his entire body had gone numb. He grasped the detonator in his one good hand and rolled over on his back to see that the dazzling light was still a couple hundred yards away. It was right beside the arsenal storage now, but coming ever nearer. Hawker had to use his chin to force open the spring-locked cover, and he fumbled for a moment trying to find the toggle switch before hitting it. There was a split-second of nothing followed by a stupendous explosion.

Everything seemed to go off at once, the plastic explosives on the houses and storage warehouses, the thermite bombs and plastic explosives in the arsenal setting off all the munitions and rockets—an earth-shaking, deafening, blinding explosion that threw a fireworks display into the night sky.

And in the initial blinding white light, Hawker watched the tank flip heavily up into the air and burst into flames as it hit the ground.

Dizzy, he tried to get to his feet. He stumbled and fell. Then someone was beside him, taking him by the right arm, urging him along. It was Sha. Behind her, looking very small, was Sarah Billings.

His voice sounding strange and very far away, Hawker said, "What are you two doing here? Get up the mountain! Get out of here!"

But the woman got her shoulder under his arm, forcing him to his feet, urging him along. And then he was actually moving on his two good legs, jogging along on instinct, following the two females blindly.

Later he would remember almost nothing about the trip up the mountain, except that they had stopped once so Sha could tape something to his shoulder, something she said would slow the bleeding. But now they moved in total darkness, through caves, over rocks, the whole thing a blur as he went along like a man on drugs.

Somehow—he would never know for sure how the girl and Sha did it—they got him to the beach and into the inflatable boat before he passed out. He awoke only once, aware of dark waves rolling toward his face, then a feeling of

being lifted as they swept beneath the boat.
Sarah seemed to be talking into something—
the radio? Yes, the radio. Yelling something
about a helicopter she needed, about where
the helicopter should meet them.

Hawker let his head slide backward as she
continued to yell into the radio and saw something lifting and rolling on the dark near hori-
zion. He tried to focus on it.

An island?

Yes, it was an island.

Maybe it was the one where they had spent
those few days—the island on which Sha had
built the jungle hut. Yes, that was it, the place
Sha longed to return to so that she could be
with him, a man and a woman, alone, away
from all the ugliness that had come close to
destroying her life.

Watching the island rise and fall, getting
ever closer, James Hawker let his eyes close, a
faint smile on his face. Whether he was dreaming or dying and approaching heaven, he
couldn't say.

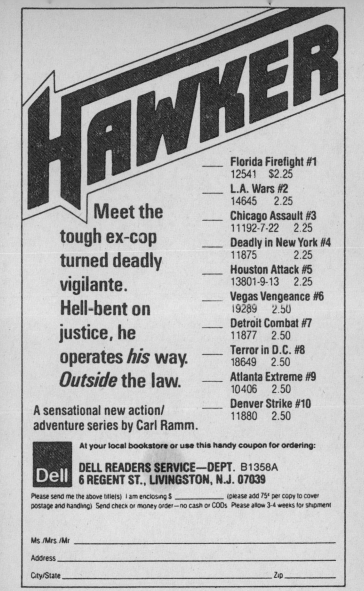